THE ASSASSIN

HARRY STARKE GENESIS BOOK 3

BLAIR HOWARD

CONTENTS

Chapter 1	1
Chapter 2	8
Chapter 3	19
Chapter 4	32
Chapter 5	40
Chapter 6	47
Chapter 7	55
Chapter 8	60
Chapter 9	71
Chapter 10	76
Chapter 11	82
Chapter 12	93
Chapter 13	97
Chapter 14	105
Chapter 15	108
Chapter 16	113
Chapter 17	116
Chapter 18	119
Chapter 19	125
Chapter 20	130
Chapter 21	143
Chapter 22	149
Chapter 23	155
Chapter 24	167
Chapter 25	172
Chapter 26	179
Chapter 27	192
Chapter 28	202
Chapter 29	207
Chapter 30	216
Chapter 31	227

Chapter 32	236
Free Book	245
Acknowledgments	247
One More Thing	249

Copyright © 2019 Blair Howard

The Assassin by Blair Howard

All rights reserved. No part of this publication may be reproduced, stored in a retrieval system, or transmitted in any form, or by any means, electronic, mechanical, photocopying, recording, or otherwise, without the express written permission of the publisher except for the use of brief quotations in a book review.

Disclaimer: The Assissin is a work of fiction. The persons and events depicted in this novel were created by the author's imagination; no resemblance to actual persons or events is intended.

Product names, businesses, brands, and other trademarks referred to within this book are the property of the respective trademark holders and are used fictitiously. Unless otherwise specified, no association between the author and any trademark holder is expressed or implied. Nor does the use of such trademarks indicate an endorsement of the products, trademarks, or trademark holders unless so stated. Use of a term in this book should not be regarded as affecting the validity of any trademark, registered trademark, or service mark.

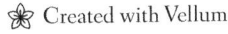

❦ Created with Vellum

For Jo, as always

1

The sun had just crawled below the horizon, and what was left of its light painted the sky orange, purple, and red. All was quiet, all but the sounds of birds chirping in the trees and cars honking on the highway beyond...

What was that? Tommy Biscotti froze and stood motionless for a long moment. The breeze was cool on his face. *Whew... Nothin'. Prob'ly just a tree branch swingin' in the wind. Yeah, that's what it is.*

He ducked through a hole in the chain-link fence that guarded the abandoned railroad tracks and made his way slowly across the dark, overgrown parking lot, a sea of broken glass and trash spread across the cracked asphalt. It was darkening quickly, but there was still enough light in the multi-colored sky to see where he was going. Tommy stepped lightly around the debris. He paused, listened, scratched his arms and sniffed the air like a wary hound. Cool as it was, he was sweating profusely, his body twitching. He moved on toward his goal.

Tommy wasn't a model citizen, but he wasn't a bad

kid, either. Average, in school and in life. He never knew his father, and his mom passed away when he was fifteen. After that his grandma took care of him, or let the TV do the job for her. That is until she'd sold it to afford some prescription meds, by which point Tommy was hooked on the high himself.

Hammerhead, Hammerhead, Hammerhead, he muttered, as if practicing a spell. For all intents and purposes, Tommy might have been trying to summon a genie, but no such luck.

He reached the first in a long line of warehouses and banged on the metal door.

"Hammer! Hammerhead! It's me, Tommy!"

The banging echoed inside. Tommy grabbed at the doorknob still warm from the sun and pulled—nothing. Locked. Probably welded, like so many of these warehouses after the local businesses left Hangar Town. Tommy crab-walked with his back to the building wall, making his way to the next door. He was shivering, or was he sweating? He swiped at his brow and confirmed that yeah, that's what he was. He pulled the sleeve of his hoodie over his left hand and wiped his face. He had to look at least somewhat presentable, and maybe this time, Hammer would give him a discount. With a bunch of crumpled bills clenched in his right hand, Tommy banged on the next door.

"Hammerhead! It's—"

The door slowly swung open, and darkness welcomed him.

If you gaze long into an abyss...

Where was that from? Something he'd half-heard back in school. How did the saying go... Ah, who really gives a—

He stepped through the open doorway into the damp, stuffy darkness... and he found it oddly comfortable. The metal door squealed shut, and then there was silence, broken only by the sound of slowly dripping water somewhere on the far side of the vast, empty space: drip... drip... drip...

"Hello?" His voice echoed back at him, surrounding him. He shook off the feeling of impending doom that threatened to overwhelm him. For a minute, he considered turning and running, but his need got the better of him.

He remembered vaguely how to get to Hammerhead's office, if you could call it that. Josie had taken him there once, a few weeks—months?—back, and together they'd navigated the maze of warehouses and garages.

A rat hissed in the corner and scuttled away, and Tommy followed it. He had to go deeper, that much he knew for sure.

He shuffled on, dodging debris illuminated by dim light spilling in through cracks and holes in the walls.

He climbed through one of those holes in the far wall, back to the outside, and looked around. An alleyway was a generous word for the narrow space between the buildings made even narrower by rusty overflowing garbage containers. There was a metal ladder that Tommy remembered climbing the last time he was there. Yes, a black ladder next to the graffiti of a shark. Bingo. Tommy swallowed and ran to the ladder.

The climb was easier than he'd expected, and a few seconds later he pulled himself up onto the warehouse roof. The wind was cooler up there, and he took a few breaths as he observed Hangar Town from this new vantage point: rows and rows of empty buildings, like a ghost town, which it was.

It was almost dark.

Tommy hurried across the roof, past more empty bottles and used syringes, until he reached the door that led downstairs. It was unlocked. In fact, there was no handle at all, just a round hole. Tommy put three fingers into the hole and pulled the door open.

He could sense he was getting closer. Any other day he'd have been excited to go on this treasure hunt, but that night he needed a dose, and that compulsion suppressed all other emotions.

He descended several dusty flights of concrete stairs and came to a door that took him into another warehouse, one that was obviously in use: pallets of cardboard and huge rolls of clear plastic were stacked against the walls. The central area was a maze of crude metal shelving. Most of the shelves were empty, but some held an assortment of old fax machines, printers, and hundreds of pieces of outdated office equipment, most of which, Tommy figured, were probably worthless.

"Hammer?" he called. No answer.

He walked the now familiar aisles, searching his memory for the way... and then he saw it: a door with a thin strip of light showing beneath.

"Ham," Tommy said, barely above a whisper, as he was about to knock on the door. He didn't.

He could hear voices within, low voices, men's voices, men who were speaking too fast for him to understand. But then he heard Hammer's unmistakable laughter—a low, rumbling sound that seemed to shake the walls.

Tommy knew he shouldn't interrupt.

He looked down at his hands. They were trembling,

but before he could do anything about it, his body seemed to move of its own volition. He grabbed the handle, twisted it, and shoved the door open.

"Hammerhead!" he shouted, and then he saw the men.

They all turned to look at him. Hammerhead stared at him. Hammer's creepy sidekick, standing at a table in the corner sorting something—something Tommy needed real bad—stopped what he was doing and looked at his boss. The other two men showed no emotion. One, who had a gun in a holster at his waist, backed away a little and looked at the other. The other guy, obviously the alpha of the two, shot a look at Hammerhead and slowly shook his head.

"And we were doing so well, weren't we?" he said and turned his head to look at Tommy.

And Tommy knew without a doubt that he was in deep trouble. He knew the kind of people Hammerhead dealt with, and he knew how those people reacted when they weren't happy. He hesitated only for a second, then backed out through the open door and pulled it shut.

"After him," someone shouted, but Tommy was already running down the aisle between the shelves, sweeping crappy old printers off the shelves as he ran.

BANG!

The sound of the shot shattered the silence and echoed around the rafters overhead, and Tommy ran, faster, up the concrete stairs, one flight, another…

BANG!

He wasn't sure if he'd been hit or not, and it didn't matter. Suddenly, he felt so alive, full of energy, especially in his legs.

"Please!" Tommy screamed to no one in particular.

He flew through the door out onto the roof and kept running. Almost at the ladder—

BANG!

He didn't feel the pain, not right away, but he did feel his body twist in the air, as if someone had just punched him hard on his left shoulder. He was still running when the bullet slammed into him, and he staggered onward, propelled by the impact, past the ladder and over the edge...

Like a bird in flight, he experienced a moment of weightlessness... and then he crashed into what felt like a pile of soft pillows. He grunted. There was the pain in his shoulder. And wetness. And warmth, no... heat was more like it. His shoulder was on fire!

He heard footsteps running, somewhere above. He scrambled around in the garbage bags and somehow made it to the edge of the container, then clambered out, his shoulder burning, and landed on the ground. His legs were still working, better than ever, so he hauled ass, taking off like a scared rabbit, along the narrow alley between the two warehouses. He held his now limp left arm across his body with his right hand soaked in blood. *Oh shit!* he thought. *That's not good... It's not fair... I didn't do nothin'.*

BANG!

The bullet ricocheted off a wall with a bright yellow spark, and Tommy snuck through a hole in the wall into a warehouse, hoping his pursuer would lose him. It was a forlorn hope.

In the darkness once again, but with the adrenaline still coursing through his veins, still doing its job, he crossed the wide-open space in what felt to him like three steps, and then he was outside again, running.

It was almost dark now in the parking lot, and Tommy felt glass and weeds crunch and rustle under his feet as he ran. Almost at the fence now... *Safe soon...* And then he froze. *What the hell was that? Who the hell is that?*

BANG!

He felt the pain now, somewhere in his body. Then everywhere...

BANG!

The impact threw Tommy to his knees.

Wetness. Warmth.

And then Tommy saw it, and he smiled. No, it wasn't an anyone, just a tree branch swinging in the wind beyond the abandoned railroad. Finally, the darkness overtook him.

2

I cracked open two bottles of Blue Moon beer and carried them out onto the patio where Bob Ryan was chilling on a chaise. I handed him one of the bottles, took a swallow from the other, and stood for a moment looking out over the great Tennessee River toward the Thrasher bridge.

The moon was up, turning the surface of the water into a shimmering expanse of silver pierced by orange spears from the lights on the bridge. It was a beautiful evening, but still chilly even though spring was in the air.

"Where the hell is she?" Bob asked, taking a sip of his beer.

I sat down next to him in a wicker chair Kate had bought at IKEA a few years back.

"She's on her way. Apparently, she was called out to a murder."

"Some things never change, huh?" he said.

"Not in this town."

"Anything there for us?"

"Not that I know of," I said, and I took a sip of my beer.

There'd been little excitement for us, for my agency, over the last couple of months. Mostly we'd worked small, routine cases—domestics—a wife who thought her husband was cheating on her, a father looking for his estranged son, several cyberattacks... You get the idea. Nobody was happy about it, least of all Bob, who had become my right-hand man and top investigator over the four years since he'd joined the agency. It had been a wild ride, those four years, and there are stories I could tell... and I might even tell them one of these days, but not now.

That night, we were sharing a few beers, loosely celebrating our four years as friends and colleagues. My business, Harry Starke Investigations, was well-established by then but, as I said, lacking excitement.

"I should've spoken to August," I said, thoughtfully, as I stared unseeing at the river. "He only takes high-profile cases these days. Maybe he could use some help. I'll call him tomorrow."

My father's an attorney, a damn good one. He specializes in those high-profile cases you see on TV: Mesothelioma, big pharma, weed killer, you know what I'm talking about, and they've made him a billionaire. My point is, August Starke has friends in high places, and we'd gotten countless cases from him over the years. *Maybe... Well, we'll see.*

My phone beeped. I picked it up, read the message, and said, "She says she's about five minutes out."

"Cool. Maybe she'll tell us about her murder," Bob said. "Hell, I'll take it pro bono if it means us getting a little action."

"I'll go grab her a beer," I said as I stood up. I took a

step toward the door and then stopped, not really knowing why.

"What is it?" Bob asked.

I shook my head. "Nothing," I said, and went on into the house.

When I was a kid, back in the '80s, I used to read superhero comic books—goofy guys with underwear over their pants, and gals wearing what could only be described as swimwear. Since then, a lot of those comics have been made into movies, and I'd seen a couple of the Spider-Man "epics." He had this thing, this sixth sense—I don't remember what it was called—his "Spidey sense," I think it was. Anyway, he would get this feeling of unease just before something bad was about to happen. I've been known to have similar feelings myself... Hell, I even see things, not often, but I do. Sometimes I can view a crime scene and... well, I see it happen, in detail. A vivid imagination? Yeah, that, probably, but the likeness of those visions to the reality is uncanny. That particular night, on my way to the kitchen, I had one of those feelings.

I'm Harry Starke, by the way. I used to be a cop, a homicide detective. Now I'm a private investigator. It's not a bad life, much the better for my getting away from the bureaucracy and BS of the Chattanooga Police Department, the CPD, where I'm still tolerated and sometimes called upon to consult on major crimes with my ex-partner, Sergeant Kate Gazzara. Unpaid, of course.

I reached into the fridge and extracted three more cold ones, put one to my forehead, and elbowed the fridge door shut. Then I heard a key being inserted into the lock on the front door.

Kate and I had been dating for almost as long as I'd

known her, more than ten years, so she had keys to my condo.

"Hey, Harry," she said as she stepped inside.

"Lieutenant." I smiled.

"Shush! Not yet. You'll jinx it."

Kate was up for promotion; she should've been promoted a couple of years prior, but she had a jerk for a boss, another reason I left the force. She was one of the best, hardest-working cops I knew, and I couldn't wait for her to get the rank she'd busted her ass to earn. Not only that, she was a lovely woman: tall, almost six feet, slim, ash-blond hair, and blue eyes that could burn a hole through a Kevlar vest.

She returned my smile and kissed me. That was my Kate: fierce and uncompromising out on the streets, but warm and loving at home. She took off her leather jacket, and I opened her beer and handed it to her.

"So, how was your day?" I asked.

"Day?" she asked, taking the bottle. "I put in almost fourteen hours. Let's just say I'm glad that it's over."

I held her close for a moment, then escorted her out to the balcony.

"Hey, Kate," Bob said, standing up and gifting her with a quick hug.

I let Kate take the wicker chair, and we all drank to my agency's anniversary. It had been an exciting four years, and I was glad to be spending the evening with the two most important people in my life.

"So, Kate," Bob said. "Anything exciting happening out there in the world?"

Bob's an ex-Chicago PD cop. He's also a marine—there's no such thing as an ex-marine, Semper Fi—and he's been with me almost since the day I first opened up shop. He's a year older than I am, a big man, six feet two, as am I, but at two hundred and forty pounds, all of it solid muscle, he's twenty-five pounds heavier. He also has a wry sense of humor and a penchant for violence. Great to have around should you need backup... but I digress.

"If by 'exciting' you mean gross and revolting," she replied, "then, yeah, more than enough to go around."

"Jeez," I said. "You want to talk about it?"

She sighed, sipped her beer, thought for a moment, then said, "It's pretty sad, actually. We got the call earlier tonight. Some loon had stumbled over a body down at Hangar Town."

Bob and I grunted in unison, and he smirked.

"The kid was barely twenty years old, Harry," Kate continued. "He had three bullets in his back."

I knew what she was feeling, but life on the streets... "That sucks, Kate," I said.

"Yeah, so you say," she replied. "Hangar Town! I can't wait for them to tear it all down. Can't August talk to the mayor or something?"

I smiled. "Trust me, he already has. Not that it ever works."

Hangar Town was a massive development project conceived back in 2006 and meant to become one of the largest business hubs in the state. A city-within-a-city, more than three thousand acres of warehouses and office buildings bounded on two sides by Hickory Valley Road and the Volkswagen Plant to the east, it was supposed to attract investors and companies from all over the world and take us all into a bright new future... Alas, the city wasn't quick enough to build the infrastructure, and the project stalled. Businesses, of course, weren't as slow to react: within months, most of the potential tenants had pulled out, leaving the warehouses empty and office buildings unfinished.

Fast-forward four years to 2012 and Hangar Town had deteriorated to little more than a vast ghost town of derelict buildings populated by junkies and petty crooks, the dregs of humanity engaged in just about every illegal activity you could name: drugs, prostitution, gun-running, and it all went unchecked. Oh yeah, the CPD was well aware of it, and what was going on there, but they'd need a separate division just to police the Town. It was fenced off, but when has that ever stopped anybody?

"I hate that place," Bob said.

"Yeah," I said. "I don't have any fond memories of it either."

"Aw, man, but that's where we first met," Bob joked.

I chuckled. It was true. Four years ago, shortly after I'd opened the agency, I was working a case for Judge McDowell, a friend of my father's. Long story short, I ended up getting kidnapped and beaten up by a couple of Russian mobsters. Bob Ryan came to the rescue... How the hell that happened, I still don't know. Now, he'll never let me live it down.

"Good times," he said.

"Speak for yourself," I replied.

"Anyway," Kate said, "I had to spend two hours running around that dump looking for witnesses."

"Of whom there were none, of course," I said.

"Of course," she confirmed. "Poor kid."

The conversation lapsed. We all drank. This wasn't how I'd envisioned the evening going, but then, as the saying goes, "The best-laid plans" and all that crap.

"What about you, guys?" she asked. "Any news on the work front?"

"Nothing new," Bob said. "People cheat, steal, and hurt each other. You know, business as usual. Nothing major, but something needs to happen. Not that I want people to get hurt, but…"

"I think we know what you mean, Bob," I said.

He finished off his beer, as did I.

"I'm just saying, Harry," he said. "I need some action. You do, too, I can feel it." He winked at me.

He was right, and just like he felt my need for action, I could feel his restlessness. I said, "Patience, my friend. Something will turn up. It always does."

"Geez," Kate said. "How morbid can you guys get? This is supposed to be an anniversary party, not a wake. Why don't we break out something stronger?"

She smiled, and I caught her drift.

"Scotch?" I suggested, grinning, since it was our go-to strong drink. "What about something to eat to go along with it?"

"Maybe order a pizza?" Kate said.

"I second that motion," Bob said, and then his phone rang. He glanced at the screen, a little confused. "It's Ronnie," he said.

Ronnie Hall was one of my oldest friends, from my high school years, and the guy I'd turned to for help when starting the agency. While my career had started at the CPD, Ronnie's background was in banking and finance. He was a man dedicated to his family and work, which included handling most of the office business, even after hours.

Bob answered the phone. "Hey, Ronnie. What's up?" He listened, then said, "Yeah, okay, sure." He looked up at me and handed me his phone. "It's for you."

We exchanged glances. I said, "Ronnie?"

"Hey, man. Do you have your phone turned off?"

"Yeah, that," I said. "What's up?"

"I have a possible lead, so I'm just calling to give you a heads-up. Turn your phone on. You're about to get a call; might be of interest."

"Okay," I said, having nothing better to say. "Who's the caller?"

"That's the thing, Harry, he didn't say. He rang in on the work number and demanded to talk to you. Said it was important. Has to do with some murder. He sounded serious."

"And you gave him my number?" I asked.

"Of course not! Who do you think I am? He already had it. Said he'd already tried to call you. I told him to give it ten minutes then try again."

Great, I thought, *just what I need—some fruitcake calling me in the middle of party night*. But such was the nature of my job. Besides, who knew, maybe the tip would turn out to be legit.

I said, "Thanks, Ronnie. Let's hope the guy isn't a stalker. If he is, I'll have your hide."

He chuckled and said, "Good one, Harry. Yeah, so, have a good night, let me know how it goes."

"Night, Ronnie," I said. I hung up, handed the phone back to Bob, and turned my own phone on.

"What's up?" Bob asked.

"Not sure yet," I said distractedly. "Maybe nothing; we'll see. Listen, why don't you order the pizza? I'll be right back."

I stepped into the house. Checked my iPhone. Two missed calls from an unknown number. No messages. That feeling of unease was back. I grabbed a bottle of scotch and was about to return to the patio when my phone buzzed.

I flipped the screen and answered the call.

"Harry Starke?" a voice that I didn't recognize said before I could say anything.

"Yes. Who is this?"

"It's about the dead guy in Hangar Town. The one who got whacked tonight. Know what I mean?"

I froze. The guy sounded serious.

"I'm listening," I said cautiously.

"See, I know who whacked the poor bastard. Well, I don't know exactly, but I can tell you who it prob'ly is."

"Okay. Why me? Why not the cops?"

"The cops?" The voice on the other end laughed out loud. "Are you high, dude? This is Hangar Town. We don't talk to cops."

"No, but you did call me, and I used to be a cop."

"Keyword being 'usetabe.' You ain't a cop no more, Harry Starke. You're a PI, and you're loaded."

I took a moment to think. So that was it. He wanted money.

It was no secret. I had money, and I wasn't ashamed to admit it. My mother passed when I was a teenager, leaving me a hefty inheritance, which I didn't spend on fancy cars and cocaine, so as far as I was concerned, I had nothing to hide. The guy seemed to have a plan in mind, so, I decided to skip the pretense and get straight to the point.

"Okay. Fair enough. How much?"

He paused, and I thought I'd caught him off guard. Which meant he hadn't thought it through, which in turn meant it could go one of two ways: first, he would name a small price, enough for a dose of his poison of choice;

second, he would get greedy and difficult. Either way, what did I have to lose?

Finally, the guy said, "Lemme sleep on it, and I'll call you back, okay?"

"When? Tomorrow? Next week? No deal. Spill it now or stop wasting my time."

I poured myself a drink.

"You testin' me, dude? I don't give a rat's ass 'bout that dead kid, you feel me? You gotta be grateful I'm even on the phone with you!"

The guy was getting worked up, so, despite a couple of words on the tip of my tongue, I took a deep breath, and then sipped the whisky. *Oh heavenly bottle.* It was excellent.

"Listen here, asshole," I said, calmly, quietly. "You called me because you want to make a quick buck. Am I right? Yeah, of course I am. So, either start talking, or go ahead and hang up. But if you do, I promise I'll find you and you'll regret you ever made this call, capisce? I... will... hurt... you. Bank on it. Now, talk to me."

There was a long pause, which I found useful. I listened hard and heard crickets chirping. *He's outdoors.*

"Screw you, man," he said, finally, and hung up.

I looked at the screen and took another sip of the good stuff. *Oh, well.*

I poured drinks for Kate and Bob and then walked in on their conversation; they were talking about retirement plans and summer homes, for Pete's sake.

"Quitting already?" I joked.

"Just trying to plan life, Harry," Kate said.

I passed the drinks around and said, "Well, I have some plans for you, guys." They stared, waiting, and I said, "I got a lead on that Hangar Town body, Kate. I think it could be legit."

"Oh yeah?" she said skeptically. "Do tell."

"That's the thing. I don't know yet, so we'll have to do some digging." That last comment was directed at Bob Ryan, who smiled as he tasted his drink.

"This is good stuff, Harry," he said. "And the whisky's decent, too." He grinned.

"Enjoy it, because that's all you're getting. We're going to work in the morning." I raised my glass, and they did the same.

Then I summarized my conversation with the mystery caller, and we devised a simple plan, with the tried-and-true first step of calling our tech guy, Tim Clarke, and asking him to trace the number.

Kate said, "I think I'm going to turn in for the night. I shouldn't be part of this anyway."

The nature of my job often put her in the uncomfortable position where she had to choose between her professional integrity and her desire to solve a case. That night she didn't seem... well, too concerned.

She stood, leaned over me, kissed me lightly on the lips—geez, did she ever taste good, and smell good too—and went inside, saying, "Do please let me know if anything comes up, okay?"

"Sir, yes, sir." I smiled, and we got to work.

3

It was after midnight, but the first thing I did was text Tim the number that had appeared on my phone. I already had an idea that the call was made from somewhere in Hangar Town, but I needed to be sure.

Tim Clarke had also been with me from the beginning and, well, I'd gotten very close to him over the last four years. He was a seventeen-year-old kid back when I dragged him out of an internet café. He was still not yet twenty-one, though he would be in a couple of weeks or so.

Midnight or not, I knew he'd jump on the opportunity to track down a number.

"What's up, Harry?" He yawned.

You'd think Tim had gone to bed already, but I knew better. I figured he'd stayed up late playing video games, probably with the aid of an energy drink or three.

"Got a minute? I have a number I need you to run down for me."

"Like, a cell phone number?" he asked. "Hold on just... one... sec."

The rapid clicking of his mouse was followed by exaggerated gunshot sounds and a low male voice announcing, "Flawless victory!"

Tim said, "Okay, I'm with you. So, you said there's a number?"

"Yeah, I got a call just now, a possible murder case lead. I need you to find the guy."

"Done," he replied. "Just text me the digits, Harry."

"Thanks."

I hung up, then copied the number from my call log and sent it in a message. Tim replied right away: *Got it. I'll let you know*.

I put my iPhone on the coffee table and sat back in the wicker chair. In the last couple of months, I'd gotten used to spending my evenings out on the patio, mostly with Kate, but sometimes with Bob, as we caught up on work and life. But I'm rambling...

"So, you really think the tip is legit?" Bob asked.

"It could be," I said.

"Right. Well, then I better get ready..."

"We're going to Hangar Town," I announced with feigned enthusiasm, and then added, "Well, not tonight, but yes, be ready tomorrow morning, early."

Bob stood up to leave, an empty beer bottle and a whisky glass in hand. He shook my hand and said, "Happy anniversary, Harry."

"Yeah." I sipped my own whisky. "Take a cab, all right?"

"Night, Harry," he said, his voice coming from within the apartment.

I sat there with my eyes closed for about ten minutes

after he'd left, and then I went inside, rinsed the glasses, and went to the bedroom.

I undressed and slid into bed next to Kate; she was warm and already half-asleep. She turned to face me, and I kissed her lips. She'd showered, but still smelled faintly of perfume and whisky, as did I.

"Do you have to work tomorrow?" she asked.

"Some. You?"

"Maybe..."

She kissed me, and I returned the kiss, and then she put her left hand on my cheek...

∽

It turned out we both had work the next day. Kate was the first to get up. She received a call at just after seven. It seems they'd found the kid's grandmother and were bringing her in for questioning.

"Do they really need you there?" I asked, rolling over in bed. It was nice and warm, and I wished for nothing else but for Kate to crawl right back in next to me.

"They might not need me, but I want to be there."

"Of course you do," I said. "Go get 'em, tiger."

I waited until she left, then showered, dressed, poured coffee for myself, and then checked my phone. Tim had left a couple of messages during the night, but I'd been preoccupied, and then we fell asleep, so...

Anyway, I scanned through the messages and learned that the phone number was for an old payphone in Hangar Town. *Geez, I didn't know there were any of those things left, let alone still in working order, especially in the Town.*

The payphone was located right next to the abandoned railroad tracks. They'd planned to build a railroad hub for the complex, but that, of course, never materialized either.

I thumbed a reply to Tim—*Thanks*—and then I forwarded his messages to Bob, counting on him being awake and ready to get on it. He was, and he called me right back.

"So, are you coming, or what?" he said.

"Not right away."

I'd thought about it last night. We'd need to canvas the crime scene area as soon as the CPD was done with it, but that wasn't going to be my first destination.

"I need you to go and check out the crime scene," I said. "That is if the PD's finished with it. If not, do a little recon and I'll join you there in a couple of hours, Bob. I got places to be."

"Oh, yeah?"

"Yes. Somebody gave that kid my number, right? And if it wasn't Ronnie, then who? As far as I'm concerned, there's only one answer to that question."

"Benny Hinkle," Bob said.

"Bull's-eye. I'm going to the Sorbonne, then I'll be with you."

"Good luck with that."

I hung up, ready to take the day by storm. I was in the zone, experiencing that first wave of excitement that always comes with a new investigation. Could it be a dud? Sure, it could, but any activity beats doing nothing, right?

The Sorbonne... Where do I even start? Yeah, the name suggests some bohemian gentlemen's club or a fancy French restaurant, right? Wrong! Sorry to disappoint you, but the Sorbonne is one of the sleaziest watering holes in town... and I love it. Its clientele consists of mostly lowlifes and drunks, and I wouldn't recommend you take a date there, but... Yes, I'm a regular at the place and I probably hang out there way too much—especially if you ask Kate—but the Sorbonne has always been instrumental to my line of work. I like to keep my ear to the ground, and there's no better place in the city for that than what Benny Hinkle is proud to call his "club."

It was just after nine when I pulled up to the curb at the rear of the Sorbonne, on a narrow alley optimistically named Prospect Street, and stared for a moment at the dirty green metal rear door.

I exited my Maxima, locked it, and then banged on the door and waited. Benny had installed a security camera above the door a while back, so I stared up at it, frowning, imagining Benny staring right back at me through some crappy black-and-white monitor. That is, if he wasn't sleeping. I banged on the door again.

"Open up, Benny, we gotta talk!"

There was a long moment of silence, then the sound of multiple locks being turned, and then the door opened. It wasn't Benny standing there, it was Laura.

"'Sup, Harry?" she said. I could tell she was not exactly thrilled to see me at that early hour.

Laura Davies was, and still is, Benny's long-time business partner, waitress, and barkeep. I like to think their arrangement is strictly business. At least I hope so, for Laura's sake, because she's married with two kids. She's a good-looking woman—tall and blond, nice figure, and usually dressed for the tips: tank top and cut-off jeans that did little to hide her... assets? Whatever. That morning, however, she wore a shapeless hoodie and black sweatpants with the word PINK down the side.

"Laura?" I said. "You look... different."

Note to self: don't ever say those words to a woman again.

She glared at me, shook her head, then said, "What the hell d'you want, Harry? Do you have any idea what time it is?"

"Er... yeah! I do. Is Benny in? I need to talk to him."

"You and everyone else," she said as she stood aside for me to enter. "Come on in."

I stepped inside, and together we walked the tunnel-like passageway to the bar where I was met by the sounds of George Jones's "He Stopped Loving Her Today" playing through the raspy old speakers. It wasn't my go-to genre, but it was definitely an upgrade from the mind-numbing garbage Benny usually served during open hours.

"Why are you here this morning, anyway?" I asked as we walked into the darkened barroom.

"Somebody's gotta do the books, Harry," she replied with a smirk.

"You mean 'cook the books,' right?'" I said with a smile.

I'd always assumed that Benny's bookkeeping was... creative, but I was surprised to hear that Laura was the artist... or not. Probably a smart decision.

"Where is he?" I asked.

"He was here a minute or so ago... probably in his office."

"Thanks, Laura," I said, and headed back down the passageway to Benny's office.

I knocked on the door. It opened immediately.

"Whadaya want, Harry?"

Benny Hinkle is not the most attractive man on the

planet: overweight, unshaven, and generally untidy, he looked like he had just woken up from a month-long slumber. Maybe he had.

"I'm not in the mood to fool around, Benny, so let's make this quick. You gave my private phone number to some methhead. Why'd you do that?"

"Huh?" He turned away, walked around his desk, and dropped his ass into his worn faux-leather chair, which in turn let out a fair impression of a pig breaking wind as the air was forced out of it.

I followed and stood uncomfortably close to him. "What the hell were you thinking, Benny?"

"I don't know... It wasn't my best moment. I'd had one too many, okay?"

"No, Benny, not okay."

I really wasn't angry, but I needed to intimidate him; I needed him to tell me who he gave it to.

"Who's the kid, Benny?"

"I can't just give you my sources, Harry," he said plaintively.

"Sources? What d'you think you are, Benny, a damn journalist?"

"Nah, but my word is still worth something on the street, ain't it? An' if it gets out I'm a snitch... well, you know."

I hesitated for a moment, wondering whether to pay him or beat it out of him. I decided on the former and took out my wallet.

Benny was an SOB, but he was also street-smart enough to get what was his. I took out a twenty and waved it in front of his nose.

"All I need is the kid's name."

Benny grabbed the bill and stuffed it into a pocket.

"First name's Jake. Last name is extra."

"Jake Extra?" I said without humor, as I produced another twenty.

Benny smiled happily as he grabbed the bill and said, "Nice doing business with you, Harry. His name's Jake Burke."

I nodded, then turned and walked out without another word, satisfied, but not happy. I went back to the bar, stood for a moment and texted the name to Tim. I didn't need to explain. He knew what to do. Then I said goodbye to Laura, and I left the Sorbonne. My visit there had been productive, and I had a feeling it would turn out to be the high point of the day, because from there I was headed to Hangar Town.

Before leaving, I texted Bob as I got in behind the wheel of my Maxima.

You know that one part of your town everyone says you should try to avoid at all costs? Well, that's what Hangar Town had become by 2012. I didn't want to leave my car anywhere near the warehouses, so I parked out of view on the side of the road and opted for a short hike cross-country.

I walked through some bushes and then down a slope through the underbrush until I reached the railroad tracks. The place didn't look too bad during daylight hours, at least what I could see of it: a rutted, overgrown parking lot and a row of unremarkable though dilapidated commercial buildings beyond. I spotted Bob at the far side of the lot near a light pole, leaning against his car, arms folded, head down, with his legs crossed at the ankles and his backside on the edge of the hood. I hiked on over.

The yellow crime scene tape was still attached to the

pole, and there were several markers around a pool of dried blood.

"So, they're still not finished then?" I said.

"Yeah, they're done. They just didn't bother to clean up... Hell, why would they?"

"This is where they found the body?" I asked.

He nodded. "Yup! I guess. If the gunshots weren't fatal," Bob said, "the guy sure as hell died from the loss of blood."

"Shame," I said, and meaning it.

"How was your visit to Benny's?" he asked.

"I'm out forty bucks, but it was worth it, if the fat little SOB wasn't lying to me, and if he was..." I shook my head, then said, "What about you? Did you find anything?"

He nodded, pushed himself up off the hood of the car, and motioned for me to follow him, and I did.

"The payphone's in working order," he said, "but that's about all. The cops have dusted it. Other than that, there's nothing so I'm not even gonna show you that. I have, however, made a tour of the premises, and I think I've established some geography. You want to see?"

"You bet!"

We left his car where it was and walked to one of the warehouses. The door was unlocked. We stepped inside. The interior was dim, lit only by a strip of narrow windows high above, and I was immediately transported back to that day four years ago when I woke to find myself tied to a chair and helpless. It wasn't a good feeling.

The warehouse was empty, the atmosphere within dusty, stuffy, oppressive.

I noticed several more yellow police markers on the floor. Each marking a drop of blood: a trail we followed across the warehouse to a hole in the wall. We climbed through it, out into a narrow alley that separated one building from another. Garbage containers lined the graffitied walls. I glanced first one way, then the other.

"This way, see?" Bob said. "More markers."

"The kid didn't go down easy, did he?"

"No, he didn't," he said. "Look, bullet holes in the wall here, and here, but... Okay, hold up a sec." We stopped. "The trail of blood ends, or rather begins, here."

I looked around, saw nothing but a rusty metal ladder leading up to the roof of the second warehouse, and from there... who the hell knew?

Knowing Bob as I did, though, I was pretty sure he knew.

"So, you think the kid got into trouble up there on the roof? A drug deal gone wrong, maybe?" I asked, then continued without waiting for him to answer. "So he takes off running, climbs down... and, what? The other guy starts shooting?"

Bob grinned. "Two things here, Harry. One, the kid didn't climb down... Well, not all the way; partway, I think, and then he fell. Two, he didn't get in trouble up on the roof. See this?" He pointed to a small, but highly stylized drawing of a shark on the wall beside the ladder.

"What is it, a new Banksy?"

"Banksy?"

"Graffiti."

"Oh, yeah?" Bob said, shaking his head. "No! It's a marker. Follow me," and he began to climb the ladder.

I followed him.

We climbed over the parapet onto the roof.

"The cops didn't follow the trail this far, because they didn't know or they couldn't be bothered, and I'm betting they didn't know. It's like you said, Harry, a drug deal gone wrong, right? Except for that wonderful example of a cave painting."

"What about it?"

"I told you, it's a marker. Come on."

We crossed the roof from one end of the building to the other.

"You ever heard of Hammerhead?" Bob asked.

"Like the shark?" I asked.

"Yeah. Hammerhead! Not the fish, Terry Lawrence, a drug dealer, among other things. These drawings are his schtick. See, here's another one."

He pointed to a spot on the wall beside a door. The door led into a small brick building at the edge of the roof that provided access to the stairs. I looked where he was pointing. It was hard to see, but it was there: small, faded, but definitely a hammerhead shark. I wouldn't have noticed it if Bob hadn't pointed it out.

"It's the only way to find him. No cell phones."

I nodded, connecting the dots. "So this Jake guy works for Hammerhead, hence his using a payphone."

Bob opened the door. It had no handle, just a hole where the handle had been.

"That's my theory," he said. "C'mon."

We went down two flights of stairs, then through another handleless door, stepping out onto the second floor of another warehouse space, with low ceilings. Unlike the others we'd seen, it wasn't empty. It was filled with rows of shelves upon some of which were stored hundreds of pieces of dusty, and mostly obsolete, office equipment. The huge room smelled of cement dust, mold, and something nasty I couldn't identify.

"Look, here." Bob pointed to a bullet hole in the wall next to the door. "Come on, there's more."

We crossed the room and stopped in front of another door.

Bob said, "I think this is where our kid got into trouble."

He swung the door open. We stepped into what must have once been a large, open-plan office space, but now it was empty, dirty, and abandoned except for a half-dozen chairs, an ancient steel desk, and a large wooden table. The desk and table both sat against the far wall. The furniture, such as it was, was clean, devoid of the dust that covered most of the rest of the room, and it was arranged in such a way that told me it had been in use until quite recently.

"A drug deal gone wrong," I said.

"That's a strong possibility," he said, nodding. "A guy, maybe two guys seated in the chairs, another sorting the goods on the table, and maybe a couple more security guys."

"Hmm." I walked over and sat down at the desk and swiveled to face the room.

"So, I'm Hammerhead," I said.

Bob sat opposite me. "And I'm the kid."

I pointed at the table. "And that there is Jake the Midnight Caller?"

"Possibly."

"Okay," I said. "So, you walk in over there, where we came in. You're here to score. You hand me some cash, and Jake hands you a dose, right?"

Bob nodded. "But then maybe I didn't give you enough, or maybe you shorted me, and we argue, and you're pissed off and decide to go after me."

I thought about it. It sounded wrong. "No, I don't think so. These guys have a rep to maintain. For all anyone knows, I took your money and shot you in the back. Bad word of mouth. Not good for business."

"Agreed," Bob said. "So, I wasn't buying anything yet, but I was going to."

"Except," I said thoughtfully, "I was already dealing with someone else... and..."

"And I interrupted," Bob added. "I'm a junkie with a burning need, so I just busted in and..."

I smiled. "And you saw my buyer, who didn't like that, and—"

I was interrupted by the sound of the door opening. We had a visitor.

4

We froze for a moment. Our visitor was huge, the size of a house.

Now, Bob and I aren't small guys—at over six-feet-two and more than 200 pounds apiece. We'd rarely had trouble taking on even the largest opponents, but our new friend was something else. His torso filled the doorway completely, and he had to lower his head to get through the opening.

He stood motionless, staring at us with large black eyes, unblinking.

"Who the hell are you?" he bellowed in a voice that seemed to shake the warehouse walls.

"More to the point, who the hell are *you*?" Bob said, getting up.

Not Hammerhead, then, I thought.

The giant didn't reply. Instead, he took a step forward, glanced at the desk, then at me.

I swiveled my chair, pulled open the top drawer, and looked inside. I smiled when I saw the small canvas pouch secured at the top by a zipper.

"You looking for this?" I asked, holding it up as he started across the room.

"Give it to me and I won't hurt you," he said, clenching his fists.

"First," I said, "tell me who you are."

Bob didn't move, and I was waiting for whatever would happen next. We'd been in similar situations before, and we'd handled most of them quite easily, but this guy... Well, he looked like he could be... problematic.

The giant obviously wasn't much of a talker, because instead of a reply, he swung a fist the size of a basketball at Bob. Speed wasn't his forte, either, and Bob exploited his lack of it with glee. As the giant swung his fist back, Bob jumped at him, delivering a gut punch that almost knocked the air out of his opponent... Almost.

Unfortunately, the punch didn't stop the man's swing; momentum took care of that, and his fist hit Bob on the shoulder, hard enough to sweep him aside and leave me exposed.

My plan was simple, and elegant in its execution. I simply braced myself in the chair and drove my foot into his groin, effectively folding him in half as I rolled out of his way. He howled in pain, but he still didn't go down. He took two more unsteady steps toward me, and then Bob got back in the game. Bob slammed a six-foot length of two-by-four down onto the middle of the huge man's back. The giant's head tipped back, and he would have been looking up into the rafters had not his eyes been closed. Another half-step and he crashed face-first onto the desk and then fell sideways to the floor, grunting.

"You okay?" I asked Bob.

"Better than this asshole." He kicked the giant in the stomach, which caused him to roll over onto his back.

I opened the pouch. Inside it was a small tin box and a small ziplock bag. The box contained a dozen joints and the baggie was packed tight with what could only be weed. A quick sniff confirmed it. I snapped the box shut.

"This is what all the fuss is about?" I asked, shaking my head.

Bob looked at me and said, "A coincidence? Wrong place, wrong time?"

"Not hardly," I replied. "Wake him up. Let's see if we can find out."

Twenty minutes later we left the giant lying on the floor of what he claimed was Hammerhead's "office." We now knew everything he knew, including his name—Russell Harris. He claimed he was there only to pick up his score. Apparently, Hammerhead had told him he'd leave it in the desk drawer for him. I believed him. Bob was right: wrong time, wrong place.

I texted his name to Kate and asked her to run it. I had a feeling the creep had a fistful of warrants out for him, but we had no time to deal with him, or hang around and wait. He'd given us Hammerhead's location, and I figured time was of the essence. Had he told us the truth? Yeah, I was sure of it. Ryan has his ways of getting people to talk, as do I.

"So, here's what I think happened," I said as we walked back across the roof to the ladder. "Jake was here with Hammerhead dealing with a customer when Tommy Biscotti crashed the party, agreed?"

"Uh-huh, and the buyer doesn't like witnesses, so he went after him," Bob said.

"And he shot him dead? Bit extreme, don't you think?"

"Probably already hopped up," Bob replied.

"Maybe, but suppose he wasn't... Hmm, I wonder if Kate has any word on the weapon. Might be useful to know what it was. Hold on a sec while I text her." And I did.

"You're right," Bob said, scratching his ear. "It isn't normal behavior. Not for your average junkie out to score a hit."

"Right," I nodded. "Which means the buyer didn't want to be seen, which also means—"

"That he's known," Bob interrupted me.

"And that means—"

Again, he interrupted me, "He doesn't like to leave witnesses, which also means—"

My turn to interrupt him: "That he's likely to clean up the rest of his loose ends and... You know what? I think we'd better get to Hammerhead ASAP, before he does."

"Agreed!"

It took no more than a couple of minutes for us to get back to where Bob had left his car.

We arranged to meet back at my office and go from there. Bob drove away. I crossed the parking lot at a run, climbed through the chain link fence, crossed the railroad tracks, and ran up the slope through the trees and, much to my relief, found my car exactly as I'd left it.

From my offices on Georgia, it was just a short, two-mile drive to the address Russell Harris had given us but, just as it always does when you're in a hurry, I felt like it took a whole lot longer to get there than it should have.

Hammer's abode was a rickety old Cape Cod with chipped paint and a patchy front lawn. *Why am I not surprised?*

We pulled into the overgrown driveway and parked

next to a 1980s Dodge Caravan that had seen better days. Then we sat for a moment, watching the house.

"D'you think he's in there?" Bob asked.

"Yeah."

"Alone?"

I shrugged. "Probably, but who the hell cares? Let's go."

We stepped out of the car, closed the doors quietly, and stood for a moment, listening.

"You hear what I hear?" I asked.

He nodded. "Yeah. It's quiet. Too quiet. Maybe he's taking a nap."

I didn't think so, but I didn't need to say it out loud. I knew Bob was thinking the same as I was. *If he is taking a nap, it's probably the last he'll ever take.*

"Let's check the back of the house," I said.

We walked across what was left of the front lawn, past the front porch whereon sat a shabby leather couch and a couple of folding lawn chairs. We turned left along the north side of the house, then left again to the rear door.

I mounted the three concrete steps while Bob stayed back, his hand on the butt of his Sig .45. I grabbed the doorknob and turned it slowly, trying not to make a noise. It wasn't locked.

In the movies, you see cops hesitate before entering a house without a warrant. They exchange looks with one another, and one of them says, "I think I heard a scream." Probable cause? It's a bit of a stretch, but what the hell; so they go ahead and break open the door.

Bob and I weren't cops, but we hesitated just the same, but not because we didn't have a warrant: we didn't need one. But only fools rush in, right? I slid my trusty

Smith & Wesson out of its shoulder holster, looked at Bob, and nodded. He drew his compact Sig 1911 forty-five from its sticky holster in the waistband of his pants, and only then did I push the door open with my foot and step cautiously inside.

It was quiet, so quiet you could almost feel it. We moved slowly along what once had been a nicely decorated hallway, then stepped into the open kitchen-living room area. It was a mess: cupboards open, chairs overturned. Bad sign.

We cleared the ground floor, then I led the way upstairs. The upper floor was also in disarray. I pushed open a bedroom door: more overturned furniture, broken glass, and... The wreckage was much the same as on the ground floor, but for one small detail: there was a dead man seated in an armchair.

"Hammerhead," Bob said.

"I'd say so," I said, stepping over to the corpse and placing a finger on his neck. "We're just a few minutes too late," I said. "He's still warm."

Hammerhead, if that's who it was, had a small-caliber bullet hole in the center of his forehead, another in his right temple, and a streak of red on his nose and cheek.

"Better clear the rest of this floor," I said. "I wouldn't want to think his killer is still here. That could get really nasty."

He nodded, left, and then returned a minute later.

"All clear," he said, "but the place is a ruin, turned upside down. Looks like somebody really wanted to find something."

"What were they looking for do you think?" I said.

"Drugs? Money?"

We did a quick search of the room and found neither.

If it was Hammerhead, it certainly seemed plausible someone was after his stash, but somehow, I found it hard to believe. The killing had all the signs of an execution, not a breaking-and-entering.

"I don't think so, Bob. It's classic. A double tap. A pro job. Somebody came with the express intention of taking him out, and I'm thinking it was the same shooter that took out Tommy Biscotti."

I stood in the middle of the room, scanning every inch of it. Pieces of stained wallpaper hung from the walls, and the pattern told me we were in what used to be a kid's room, maybe even little Hammerhead's, in which case...

"What do you see, Harry?" Bob asked. He had put his Sig away and waited.

"Nothing yet, but..." *Kids have secret hiding places, right?* I thought.

I walked over to the closet and opened the doors. It was full of old, nasty-looking clothes. Much as I hated to touch them, I pushed them aside, turned on my iPhone flashlight and looked around... nothing. I was about to step away when I had one of those weird feelings. I have no idea what made me do it, but I stepped inside, turned and looked up at the strip of drywall above the doors. It was a strip about eight inches wide running the entire length of the closet. And, bingo, there it was: a small section about twelve inches long, separate from the rest of the strip. Without the light, it would have been all but invisible.

"Knife?" I asked, sticking out my hand.

I heard Bob flip it open and then felt him place the shaft in my open hand. Carefully, I inserted the blade into the crack between the two sections of drywall and levered the smaller section out to reveal a small rectangular opening. I reached inside, felt around, and withdrew a ziplock bag. I ducked out of the closet and held it up to the light of the window. Inside it was a flip phone and battery.

Bob smiled. "Well-spotted, Harry. Anything else in there?"

"Nope, just this."

I took the phone out of the baggie and checked it out—it was dead; the battery had been removed. I returned it to the baggie, stuffed it into my pocket, then went back inside the closet and replaced the section of drywall. Then we left the bedroom and headed for the stairs.

"We'd better let Kate know about Hammerhead," Bob said.

"Of course, just as soon as we're out of here."

We went downstairs and exited through the front door. I backed the car out of the driveway, drove a couple of blocks on down the street, and parked.

I took the flip phone from the plastic bag and opened it. It was a relic from the good old days when cell phones were just that—phones, not supercomputers. I replaced the battery and turned it on.

I thumbed through the phonebook, which took no time at all; the thing only held ten numbers. I found the name I was looking for, "JB." *Jake Burke*. Next, I checked the call log.

Hammerhead didn't use the phone often. His main interest was his supply line—drugs. His second was Jake, his right-hand man whom he seemed to be in the habit of texting every other day, mostly to arrange a meet at a watering hole called the Lucky Crow.

There we go, I thought, smiling to myself.

I texted Jake, *lucky crow, 15min*, and hit *Send*, and then turned the phone off and removed the battery.

5

The Lucky Crow turned out to be a grubby pool bar that could've given Sorbonne a run for its money, at least that was the way it looked from the outside.

We parked across the street, and I left Bob in the car to watch the front and talk to me through an earpiece.

"Mike check, mike check," I said, as I crossed the street.

"Loud and clear, boss."

"Zip it, Ryan," I said. He knows how I hate being called "boss." That being so, it's become a joke that never gets old, at least to him and the rest of the team.

I pushed through the door into a room the size of a football field, a wide-open space divided into two sections: the first, taking up almost two-thirds of the space, contained a row of six pool tables. The other third was a "lounge"—and I use the word loosely—with a dozen small round tables and half-dozen seats set around a semicircular bar behind which two guys—bartenders—were loafing together, leaning on their elbows on the bar top.

They both looked up when I entered, but neither of them made a move.

Two of the pool tables were occupied and there were, by my count, five people in the bar watching ESPN on several flat-screen TVs.

I stepped up to the bar. The nearest of the two loafers turned his head to look at me and said, "What can I get ya, bud?"

"You got coffee?" I said.

The man shook his head. "Booze or tap water, your choice."

"Great choice. A beer, please."

He exchanged a bottle for a five and kept the change.

"I'm meeting a guy here, his name's Jake. Tell him I'm outside."

I headed outside to the patio area—again, I use the words loosely—where there were two filthy barbecue grills and a half-dozen round tables. The patio was littered with cigarette butts and bottle caps. That aside, surrounded by a tall wooden fence, the area did have a certain charm to it. I picked out a table in the corner and sat down with my back to the fence so that I could observe both the patio and a section of the interior. There was no one out there but me. I twisted the cap off of the bottle, took a sip, and set it down. Then I took out my gun and rested it on my knee.

"In position," I said. "It seems quiet. Once he's in, make sure it stays that way."

"Roger that," Bob said.

I nodded, even though I knew he couldn't see me: force of habit, I suppose.

I grabbed my beer, leaned back in my seat, and waited.

A few minutes later, Bob said, "I think I got him. Red hoodie, black jeans, long hair. I'll be at the door."

"Gotcha."

I put my hand on my gun. There were two ways this meetup could go. Either Jake would run, in which case Bob would grab him at the door and I'd have to flash my gun in public, or he'd sit down at my table and try to bluff it out. Fortunately, he chose the latter.

"Congrats, dude, you found me," he said, dropping his butt onto the seat opposite me across the table, chewing gum, smacking it in a loud and obnoxious way that scored him no points.

"How's Hammerhead?" he asked. "I hope you beat the crap out him." He grinned.

He was a wiry little white guy, maybe twenty-five years old. Skinny, with a thin face, a hook nose, and bloodshot eyes. The boy had seen some hard living, that was sure: it was about to get harder.

"Give me a minute, Jake," I said, slipping the M&P9 into my pants pocket and rising to my feet.

I had considered trying to actually talk to him, maybe even drop a couple of hundred on him for whatever info he might have had, but everything about his attitude told me he would squirm and bullshit all day before giving me anything useful. So, I decided to go on the offensive.

I went to the door, leaned in and said, "I need a little privacy out here. Okay if I close the door for a few minutes?"

The two barkeeps, still leaning on the bar, looked at each other, and then one of them nodded. I thanked him, closed the door, and returned to my seat, my gun back on my thigh.

I took a sip of my beer, looked him in the eye and said, "Hammerhead's dead."

His mouth hung open, and his brows arched, as his tiny brain processed what I'd just said.

"You killed him? What kind of psycho are you?"

"I didn't kill him, Jake. But I do have a gun under this table, aimed at your nuts. Now, your proposition is off the table, but you might still walk away in one piece."

I gave him a few seconds to figure out his only option, and then he said, "This is, like... It ain't cool, man."

"That's the idea," I said.

Bob chuckled into my ear and said, "I'm coming in."

I took out my earphone and said, "Spill it, Jake, or you're going to have a problem."

Bob joined us at the perfect moment. He shut the door behind him, blocking the door out to the patio, and I glanced at him, which made Jake also turn his head at my partner. Bob waved.

Jake said, "Okay, okay, you got me. Just promise you won't tell the cops."

"We'll see what we can do," Bob said.

"Who was there at the Town last night?" I asked.

"I don't know."

"Wrong answer, Jake."

He said, "No, seriously. I mean, some guys, two guys. I never seen either of 'em before. One of them chased Tommy and killed him, while Hammerhead sold dope to the other. Pills."

"What kind of pills?"

"Adderall," Jake said. "Two bags of it, a thousand pills, man."

"Adderall?" Bob asked as he joined us at the table.

"Aren't they the pills that medical students pop to help them study?"

Adderall is used to treat attention deficit disorder, but college kids often turn to them to stay focused while studying long hours. It can be taken orally or the pills can be ground to powder and snorted. It was a bitter irony that it did indeed help many young people graduate, only to end up hooked on the drug.

"I'm guessing these guys weren't med students, right?" I said.

"Nah, man. But only one of 'em looked like he needed the dope, you know? He was, like, nervous, tapping his foot and shit."

"You're doing great, Jake," Bob said.

"Yeah," I agreed. "Now, what did they look like? Did you hear any names?"

"I did. The main guy called the oth—"

What happened then was surreal. Jake's head exploded. There was no loud bang or any other indication of a shooter, just a loud smack as the bullet impacted the back of Jake's head and exited through his left eye socket.

Blood and brain matter flew everywhere, on me, Bob, the table, as the force of the hit threw Jake's body forward, out of the chair, onto the table, dead even before he hit the floor like a sack of potatoes.

Instinctively I reacted, jumped to my feet, twisting, rolling, trying to see where the shot came from. I caught a glimpse of a shadowy figure—just the head and shoulders—on one of the low roofs more than a hundred yards away.

"Call Kate!" I ordered as I ran to the fence.

Bob was already on it, so I cleared the fence and ran down the alley. The figure stood up, outlined against the blue sky, holding what looked like a long black tube. It could only have been a sniper rifle. The figure ducked and began to run, bending low, across the roofs. I sprinted onward in the direction of the building where the figure had disappeared, my gun still in my hand.

Breathing hard, I jumped onto the hood of a parked car, then onto its roof, and there I had to pause. I needed both hands to climb from the roof of the car onto the canopy over the door of the building, and from there up onto the roof.

I holstered the gun, made the leap, and then clambered up onto the flat roof where I found... nothing. No one.

I took my gun from its holster and moved cautiously across the roof in the direction I'd seen the shooter run.

I heard police sirens howling in the distance. They'd be heading for the Lucky Crow which meant, I hoped, I wouldn't be confused with the perp and taken down. That'd be a way to go...

I reached the parapet at the far end of the roof and looked over and down, and I spotted him running across the street. I took careful aim, but before I could shoot, he hopped into a white panel van and, with tires squealing, it took off, even before the door had closed.

"Freeze!" I shouted out of the old habit from my CPD days, and I fired three shots, two hit the side panel of the van, third took out one of the rear door windows. And then it was gone. Me? I stood for a minute, breathing hard, then I holstered my weapon and climbed down over the canopy and the car to the street level. I took out my ID, ready, in case someone approached me. And they did.

"Get your hands up, asshole!" I heard from somewhere behind my back.

"My name is Harry Starke. I'm a private investigator," I said, slowly raising my hands and turning.

A slender Asian woman dressed in jeans, a black leather jacket, and sunglasses was pointing a gun at my face.

"A PI? Well, hell," she said, lowered her gun, and then taking off her shades said, "My name is Agent Casey Wu."

6

She put her gun away. I lowered my hands. She stepped forward, her right hand extended; I shook it. Agent Casey Wu was... not exactly petite, maybe five-seven, slim with shoulder-length black hair and dark brown eyes. She reminded me a little of a thirty-year-old Julie Chen. Her grip was strong, almost manly, and I was close enough to her to get a whiff of perfume that made me think of white roses.

"So," I said, "what agency are you with?"

She smiled. "I'm not an agent, per se, but it does have a nice ring to it, doesn't it?"

I frowned, but agreed, reluctantly: "It does."

She said, "How about we go see what's happening back at that bar, and I'll explain."

"Did you see what happened?" I asked as we started walking back the way I had come.

"We were watching, Mr. Starke, yes. But I guess I should start from the beginning. My team and I are part of TSA. We're a security team."

I made a mental note to fact-check that later. In fact, I was listening very closely to every word Agent Wu said.

"TSA?" I asked. "You're working for the Transportation Security Administration... Airport Security? I don't believe it."

She laughed, then said, "Hardly. Tipton Security Agency—TSA—is a private security contractor to the NSA, which means we have federal authority."

"I see," I said, not yet willing to go into full grilling mode. The images of the poor kid's head exploding were still printed on my retinas, like a horrible wraith that'd stuck around to torment me.

We arrived back at the Lucky Crow, which obviously wasn't very lucky for one Jake Burke, to find Bob Ryan pacing back and forth next to my car. The bar had been cordoned off and uniformed officers were rounding up witnesses on the sidewalk.

You'd never know it, but I knew that Bob was devastated by what had happened. He was one of the toughest guys you'd ever meet, but the death of innocents never did sit well with him.

"I take it you didn't get the bastard," he said, as he sized up Wu, then looked at me, his eyebrows raised.

"Agent Wu, this is my partner, Bob Ryan."

"Agent Wu?" he asked as they shook hands.

"Well, private security. You can call me Casey," she said, looking up at Bob over her sunshades.

"And you can call me Bob. Pleasure to meet you."

He let go of her hand and turned to me. "Kate is on her way."

Wu's phone beeped. She glanced at it, then said, "Sounds like you boys have business to attend to, and so do I. Nice try back there, Mr. Starke. Pity it didn't work out. Here..." She produced a business card and handed it to me. "Call me when you're done here. I think maybe we should talk. What do you say?"

I took a moment to consider the offer. I should have stalled, kept her talking, restrained her if I had to until Kate got there. *Agent* Casey Wu, as her business card stated, was a witness, and I had a certain feeling that she knew a whole lot more than she was letting on. Which was why I said, "Sounds like a plan," and put away her card.

"Splendid. I'm looking forward to working with you both." She adjusted her sunglasses and zipped up her leather jacket—even though it was one of the hottest days that spring—and lit a cigarette.

"*Ciao*," she said, exhaling a huge cloud of smoke. And with that, Casey Wu turned, walked quickly away, and disappeared around a corner.

Bob and I stood for a long moment staring after her.

"I have more than a few questions, Harry."

"You and me both, brother... You and me both."

To be truthful, I didn't know what the hell to think. My mind was racing. What had begun as the seemingly mundane murder of a junkie in a bad part of town, now involved a series of execution-style hits and a private security force... The leader of which had obviously been watching me—us—for quite a while. And that, in itself, bothered me almost as much as the killings.

What the hell is going on?

"Outside of the airport security people, have you ever heard of TSA?" I asked.

Bob is ex-military and an ex Chicago PD cop, and he sometimes surprises me with his knowledge of all things clandestine.

"No. I guess it's an acronym for... a private security contractor?" he asked.

"Yeah, that," I said, and I would have explained, but then Kate arrived.

"I'll tell you later," I said. "You'll like it."

We crossed the street and I opened the car door for her. As I did so, a second blue-and-white pulled up behind her. The driver's side door swung wide open and Sergeant Lonnie Guest eased himself out.

Lonnie and I were at the Academy together; we've never gotten along. He's tall, overweight, and about as obnoxious and annoying as a man could be. Since Kate made Detective, he'd found every excuse to tag along and annoy her and everyone else in the vicinity.

"Hey, Starke," he said. "Why is it that every time there's a shooting, you seem to turn up?" he said, with a smirk, as if he'd just told a joke no one else was laughing at.

"Don't know, Lonnie," I replied. "Maybe because I'm out here doing the legwork, while you're just sitting on your ass eating donuts and drinking coffee."

"Harry!" Kate said sharply.

"What?"

She held up her hand, then turned and said, "Sergeant Guest, please make sure the crime scene is secure." Kate was all cop that afternoon and obviously in no mood to take friction from anyone, including me. Her ability to instantly switch modes between cop and civilian was a quality I admired, especially since it was something I found hard to do myself.

Guest disappeared into the bar, grumbling to himself, accompanied by a uniformed officer, who I could hear rattling away to him what few facts they'd been able to gather.

As soon as he was out of hearing range, Kate said, "Damn it! Talk to me, Harry."

I took her aside, and Bob and I proceeded to walk her through our most eventful day in months, up until the point I lost the shooter a few blocks away.

"White van, no plates," I said. "Two bullet holes in the driver's side panel south of the rear door, and one in the rear door window."

"You fired your weapon?" she asked, holding out her hand.

"You want my gun?" Of course she did. Stupid question.

"Dammit. Harry, this is serious," she said. "Now hand it over before I have Guest arrest you."

I did as she asked.

She looked into my eyes knowingly, and then said, "Is there something else you want to tell me?"

"Not yet," I said.

I figured that if I was going to get to the bottom of the mess, I needed autonomy; I needed to be at least one step ahead in the game. Giving up Casey Wu at this point would effectively kill my investigation. I needed to know exactly what her involvement in the three killings was, and the only way to do that was to talk to her, on her level.

"Okay," Kate said. "I know you're up to something, Harry, just... be careful."

"When am I not?" I asked with a grin.

She gave me a look, and Bob said, "I'll keep an eye on him, Kate."

"Oh geez, thanks, Bob, now I feel so much better," she said, giving him a wry look.

He grinned at her.

And she let us off the hook, mostly, I assumed, because she didn't need us, not then anyway. She had a handle on all three murders—not without our help—and they were looking for the mystery shooter in a white van decorated with bullet holes. Yeah, I'd need to make a statement and file a report, but at that moment she had more pressing matters to attend to... and so did I. For one, I had to go change my clothes, covered as they were in brain and blood spatter.

We returned to my car and I hit the starter, but before I pulled away, Bob put his hand on my arm and said, "Hold on a minute, Harry. Are you sure about what we're doing? I don't know what that pseudo-agent Wu lady told you, but I don't trust her, not one little bit... And I don't like her, either."

"Like her?" I asked. "What's not to like, apart from her smoking? Trust her? Absolutely not. But I'll be damned if I'm not curious."

"You really wanna pursue this, then, huh?"

"Like you don't? Bob, this thing is big. I have a feeling."

"Of course you do..." he said.

"That guy on the roof was a sniper, Bob. Who uses a sniper to take out a junkie? No one."

I let the engine idle, as I thumbed through my phone and brought up Tim's number and called him.

He was at the office, testing some new accounting software with Ronnie, whatever that meant. Since day one, I'd pretty much left the two of them to it, to do whatever they felt necessary to make my life, and ultimately theirs, run as smooth as possible. My management style was strictly hands-off, and it hadn't let me down yet.

I had them on speaker and quickly caught them up on the events of the past twelve hours and finished the story by asking, "Have you guys heard of TSA?"

Ronnie said, "Of course: Airport security."

I glanced at Bob and said, "No, not that. Tipton Security Agency. A contractor for the NSA."

"For real?" Tim said.

"Yeah. TSA and an Agent Casey Wu. I need to know everything there is to know about her and TSA: bios, contacts, everything. You know the drill." I heard him typing even before I finished the sentence, so I added: "But, Tim? Tread carefully. If it's legit, we might be stepping on government toes and playing with dangerous people."

"I gotcha. Anything else?"

"Make it your top priority. Bob and I are meeting Wu later today, so I need it ASAP."

Ronnie said, "You got it."

I hung up, and then fished Wu's card out of my pocket.

Bob said, "I still don't get why we're doing this, Harry. Who's our client? What are we even investigating?"

Good question, Bob, I thought. *I wish I knew the answer.*

I turned to him, not sure if he was being serious, and said, "That kid got shot right in front of us, Ryan. Hell, we practically put him right in front of the shooter and drew a nice round target on the back of his head, didn't we?"

"It wasn't our fault, Harry," he said.

"I'd like to think that, Bob, but he was there because I asked him to be... Oh hell, what does it matter now? The least we can do now is get some justice for him. Are you in or not?"

"You're the boss," he said grudgingly.

I pushed air through my nose, frustrated, but I wasn't going to make a scene. Instead, I dialed Wu's number.

I thought she wasn't going to answer, but eventually she did, "Wu."

"This is Harry Starke. Where do you want to meet?"

"Parking lot. Corner of St. Elmo and West 31st," she said without a pause. "Near the creek. Thirty minutes."

"I know the place," I said and hung up.

7

I took the long way around, hoping to give Tim enough time to do a background check on our potential new friends. He's good, but I wondered if he was good enough to produce what I needed in time for the meeting.

Of course he is!

Bob and I didn't talk as I drove. No, there wasn't any tension between us. This was work. We were both professionals, and we both needed to think. Deep down, though, I was a little taken aback by his lack of enthusiasm. It wasn't like him. Did I understand his hesitation, his lack of trust concerning Wu? Absolutely. But he had my back, so nothing else really mattered.

I drove south on Lee Highway to West 31st and turned right toward St. Elmo. I pulled up at the stop sign. I was facing a huge dirt parking lot—there are several dozen brand new condos built on it now, but back then, it was a vacant lot bounded to the north by a paved road lovingly called Sinclair Road and beyond that, Chickamauga Creek.

Just as I pulled across St. Elmo onto the lot and parked next to an eighteen-wheeler, Tim called.

"Talk to me, Tim."

"Everything checks out, Harry. It's all good."

"Everything?"

"Yup. Tipton Security Agency," he paused, chuckled, and then continued, "They're a small private security force contracted to the NSA. The owner, CEO and COO is one Cassandra Wu, American, of mixed American and Chinese parentage, thirty-five years of age. She's not technically an agent, though."

"Yeah, I figured. Anything else?"

"TSA has twelve employees, all ex-military. Her core team consists of four members, including Wu, all of them ex-special forces, except for Wu, who is ex-CIA. She formed the company immediately upon leaving the CIA back in 2006. She received her first NSA contract six months later... I'd say she has friends in high places. TSA pays its taxes, but moves around... a lot, all over the world. The exact nature of her work is unknown and rated Top Secret."

Ronnie chimed in: "I took a look at them, too, Harry. They're clean."

"Too clean?" I asked.

"Not really. They've had some run-ins with the boys in blue, but mostly small stuff—speeding tickets, expired licenses, that sort of thing."

"Got it," I said. "Thanks, guys."

To Bob, I said, "Good news, we're all clear to proceed. Sounds like TSA is clean."

Bob only shook his head, frowned, seemingly unconvinced as we stepped out of the car.

I had my iPhone in hand and was about to dial Wu,

when the eighteen-wheeler next to us came to life, hydraulics buzzing: its trailer door began to open, but instead of opening like you'd expect—two swinging doors—the door lowered, forming a ramp.

We heard steps coming from within, and then Casey Wu walked down the ramp.

"You boys lost?" she said, smiling. "Tim's good, maybe too good. He could get himself into serious trouble."

Bob and I exchanged glances as we headed for the rear of the truck.

"You heard my call?" I said, more than a little pissed off.

"I did. Nice to know we passed Tim's scrutiny. Come on in."

She turned and mounted the ramp; we followed her and the door closed slowly behind us, cutting out the sunlight and leaving us blinking in the dim candescent light.

"This is some kind of *Knight Rider* shit right here," Bob said.

The trailer was actually a high-tech mobile communications center. In the back was what I assumed to be a small sleeping area. In the middle of the "room" was a table, which we later discovered to be a touch-screen display. Seated at it were a man and a woman.

The man grinned at us and said, "Your guy, Tim, is good, Mr. Starke."

My heart sank, but I didn't let it show. Instead, I returned his grin and offered him my hand.

"That he is. And you are?"

"Donald Rockford. The brains of the operations, some might say."

We shook.

"Some might say," Wu said, "but they don't. Don is our tech guy, Mr. Starke, as I'm sure you've figured out."

Rockford said, "I detected Tim checking us out, so I figured I'd return the compliment." He turned to Bob, offered him his hand, and said, "Nice to meet you in person, Mr. Ryan."

I listened, but I was watching the other woman. She sat quietly, observing us. She couldn't be more different from Rockford. Where he was tall, white and skinny, she was taller, even seated—more than six feet by my estimation—dark-skinned, and outweighed him by a good sixty pounds; none of it fat. Her dark brown hair was tied back in a ponytail. Her blue eyes were piercing and mistrustful. She said not a word.

Casey Wu spoke for her: "That's Elona Jackson. Our muscle, *one might say*."

Elona gave us a barely perceptible nod, and that was the end of that interaction.

"What about the other one... your number four?" I asked.

"You mean Simon?" Rockford said. "Very good, Mr. Starke."

"Simon is out on a supply run," Wu said. "He'll be joining us shortly. Please, sit down." And we did, on either side of Rockford.

With a touch of his hand, he brought the display-table to life, and all I could think of was, *Geez, would Tim ever like to get his hands on one of these. I'd better not even mention it to him.*

I couldn't imagine how much the tech in that trailer must have cost, the more so when TSA's tech guy began playing with it.

Casey Wu said, "The man you pursued today, Mr.

Starke, was not just any murderer. We've been after him for more than three years, and today was the closest we've come to capturing him. I'm so sorry we couldn't save the boy you were with." She looked down at the floor and then glanced at the monitor in front of us and said, "That's him."

The monitor was displaying a black-and-white passport photograph. The man had short hair, and an eerily blank expression on his face, his dark eyes staring, seemingly at nothing.

"This man is a ghost," Wu said.

"Does the ghost have a name?" Bob asked.

The three members of TSA all frowned—the involuntary reaction you might have if you were suddenly reminded of something bad, an old enemy perhaps.

"We call him Nero," Wu said.

8

"Nero?" I said.

The man in the picture stared back at us. There was a short file—more like one of those old index cards—next to the image, and the information was minimal. I'd gotten the impression that Donald Rockford was a master hacker, much like Tim, and if this was all he'd managed to dig up, then this Nero guy really was a ghost.

"That's the code name we use," Wu explained. "Nero's English. His real name is Albert Westwood, ex-SAS, British Special Air Service. We did a mission together, back in oh-six."

Donald tapped, and a different photo appeared: a grainy image of a half-dozen soldiers, including Wu, in full battle gear. We learned later that they would soon become TSA.

"Albert was a star marksman," Wu continued, "and not just in our squad. All you had to do was show him the target, and he'd take care of it. He's a champion sniper—"

"I recognize him. That's Al Westwood?" Bob asked, interrupting her.

Everyone stared at him, me included, and he added, "Well, I've heard the name, back in my day. That guy was a legend. He's one of the good guys, or he was."

Wu nodded, and then she sat down next to us and said, "He was."

"What happened?" I asked, although I had a pretty good idea. My guess was that the same thing had happened to Westwood that happens to so many ex-military professionals: after their discharge, they're unable to accept civilian life and end up back in action as mercenaries. You could argue the reasons why: maybe the government should take better care of the vets, or maybe war rewires the brain. Who knows. More often than not, though, it's the money. An experienced soldier, especially ex-special forces, can make more in two weeks than he can in a year in civilian life.

Wu confirmed as much: "Money happened," she said. "Albert worked with us for several months, and then he was offered a lucrative contract for just a few days' work."

"A contract kill?" I said.

"A high-profile target in Eastern Europe, all expenses paid plus a hefty bonus for a quick and silent hit. More money than he would've made in a year with us working as a glorified bodyguard. Needless to say, he was on the next plane out."

"Piece of shit," Donald muttered.

She nodded. "You could say that. We still haven't gotten over his betrayal."

There was a moment of silence as the five of us stared at the photo.

"Since we're sharing," I said, "do you want to hear our theory on what happened?"

"With the kid at the bar?" Wu asked.

I studied her face, and then said, "Including Jake, yes."

When I was done with our story, Rockford said, "Adderall! Classic Nero. He would pop that stuff daily, to keep himself calm and awake. I swear, sometimes I thought he wasn't even human."

"Makes sense," Wu said.

"The only part that doesn't make sense," I said, "is that there was someone else with him."

The three TSA members exchanged glances.

Donald said, "Maybe Nero has a friend?" Even Elona, who had shown no emotion thus far, smirked at the notion.

"If so," Bob said, "I'd wager that it was the friend that killed Tommy Biscotti. Al wouldn't have blown through a half a magazine."

"Unless he was playing with him," Wu said. "Nero always did have a sadistic streak."

"Who is the other guy, though?" I asked.

Nobody answered, and then my phone rang, and I excused myself. Thankfully, the truck was big enough for me to go talk in a quiet corner. It was Kate.

"Harry, talk to me. None of this makes sense. What do you know?"

I knew this moment would come, but I wasn't quite ready to unload. I had to get my thoughts together, to regain control of the situation. So far, I'd felt like someone else was leading me around by the nose. It had turned into the Casey Wu show, and I needed to take it back.

"I'm not sure. I'll have to call you back, Kate," I said, and hung up.

I returned to the table but didn't sit down. I said, "So, the big question is: Why is he here in Chattanooga?"

Casey Wu looked at her team, then at Bob and me. She said, "Like we told you, Nero is a contract killer. High profile targets take a lot of prep time, which is what we think he's been doing for the past several days."

"Who's the target?" I asked.

"I assume you watch the news, Mr. Starke?" Wu said.

"I have a radio in my car."

"Then, you've heard of Senator Andrew Hawke?"

"Of course," Bob said.

I nodded. I knew the name, but not from the news.

"Chattanooga is, or was, his hometown," I said. "He's running for governor."

"That's true," Wu confirmed. "He's presently in Nashville. Then he's scheduled to visit Memphis, and then back here to Chattanooga where he's scheduled to give a speech at his old high school, and possibly other locations."

Yes, I knew Hawke, not personally, but through my father, August. As I mentioned earlier, August Starke is a prominent attorney, and he has many friends and connections, most of them formed during his high school and college years. Andrew Hawke was one of them. I'd met him several times, always in company with August. He was likable enough, though a politician through and through.

"Do you have a plan, Casey?" I asked.

"Nope," Rockford answered for her, then quickly glanced at his boss and added, "I mean, we've been tracking Nero for weeks, but he's unpredictable. We have a few ideas, but—"

"We could use some help," Wu said, smiling, "someone local, someone familiar with the battlefield. How about it, Harry?"

And there it was, my control of the situation, and it was practically handed to me. At the time, I thought it was a win...

I stared at her, contemplating the offer, though already knowing I was going to accept it.

"I'll tell you what," I said. "How about we wait until the rest of your team returns, and then we all take a ride to my office? There is a lot more space there."

"What about the cool factor?" Donald said with a grin, spreading his arms wide to show off his tech.

"Hard to argue with that," I said.

Wu agreed, and I gave them the address—even though I knew Donald already had it—and we decided not to waste time waiting.

Wu pressed a button on one of the wall panels and the exit ramp lowered, letting in the early evening light. The sky was a wash of pale orange and red-tinted clouds.

Back in my Maxima, Bob said, "These folks are pros, Harry, I'll give 'em that. How about that truck? Fancy, huh?"

"Yeah, they certainly make an impression. What's your read?"

"They said all the right words, as far as I could tell. They're secretive, but that's private security for you, right? Tim says they check out, and I trust him."

"Same here."

I did trust Tim, and Casey Wu did seem to know her stuff. I'd need to see her team at work, but at that point in the investigation, they knew way more about this Nero character than I did, so I wanted to keep them close. Which is why I'd invited them to meet at my offices; that and I wanted my team involved every step of the way, and that included Kate. I called her.

"Well?" she said impatiently.

"Sorry I hung up on you, Kate. Bob and I were working a lead. Can you meet us at the office in half an hour?"

"I suppose I could. Thirty minutes."

"Thanks," I said, smiling, but she'd clicked off.

"I'm glad you're bringing her in," Bob said. "I have a feeling we're going to need all the help we can get, including backup from the PD."

I nodded. He was to be proved right over and over during the coming weeks. I backed out of the parking lot, swung the car left onto 31st, then left again onto Broad Street, and headed north toward the office.

"By the way," I said. "How come you know this Nero... Westwood guy?"

"I'm a marine, Harry. Remember? Like I said, the guy's a legend."

Kate was already waiting outside when we arrived, and she looked worried.

No shit, Harry, I thought. With three dead bodies on her hands, she should be.

"How serious is it, Harry?" she asked.

"Oh, it's serious, I'd say," Bob answered for me, grinning.

I gave him a sharp look, but it had no effect on him. He just shrugged, smiled, and went through into the outer office, leaving me alone with Kate. Any other time I might have taken advantage of the moment and given her a peck on the lips, but I could tell that she was in no mood for such frivolities.

"Have you heard of TSA?" I asked, then felt dumb for asking such a stupid question.

"Of course I have—"

"I know," I interrupted her, "but let me..." And I began to bring her up to date. By the time we had gotten coffee and settled down in my personal office, I'd pretty much caught her up on Casey Wu and her team of mercenaries, and given her a heads up on what we might expect from them. I didn't let on, though, that I didn't have a clue what that might be myself.

"And they're here why?" she said.

I didn't have time to answer. There was a knock on the door and Jacque stuck her head inside.

"Harry! We thought you weren't coming!"

Jacque Hale is my PA and perhaps the most important member of my staff. She was, along with Tim and Ronnie, one of the first people I'd hired when I formed my agency. With a master's degree in Business Administration and a Bachelor's in Criminology, she's one of the smartest people you'll ever meet; she is also the heart of my operation, and she knows it. Her smile is infectious, even on that grim day.

"Hey, Jacque," Kate said.

"Hey, yourself, Miss Kate. You here to do some work, huh?"

Ten minutes later, I had everyone gather in the conference room where I laid out the facts as I knew them so far, and about Casey Wu and the Tipton Security Agency.

Tim once again confirmed that every member of her team was ex-military and was even able to confirm TSA's connection to Albert Westwood. Wu and Westwood had indeed served together on several tours to the Middle East, all of them classified operations.

"And you decided not to hack the Pentagon?" I asked with a smile.

Tim grinned at me, pushed his glasses up the bridge of his nose with his forefinger, and said, "I was going to, but he advised against it." He jerked his head at Ronnie, who grinned with me.

"He's going to get us all arrested one of these days," Ronnie said.

Inwardly, I shuddered, because Ronnie was probably right. Tim never passed on an opportunity to hack into the best-protected systems, including—I closed my eyes when I thought about it—just about every government agency you can think of: the IRS, FBI, Homeland Security... not sure about the NSA, but I wouldn't be surprised. Dangerous? Oh yeah, but... No, I'm not going to tell you it's why I hired him... Well, yes it was. I need to know what I need to know, and Tim can provide it, quickly. I trust him implicitly, and it wouldn't be the last time in the investigation that we'd need to utilize his skills.

"So there's only one thing that I find odd about TSA," Tim said, thoughtfully.

"What's that?" I asked.

"TSA has a number of vehicles in their stable—an SUV, two sedans, and, check this out, a semi-truck with a trailer."

Bob tried to hide his smile, as did I.

"Wh-at?" Tim said.

"That's their mobile headquarters."

Tim's mouth hung open. "Seriously?" he asked.

"Seriously," I said. "Maybe they'll let you take a look

around, but don't get any ideas. All right, everybody?"

My four exchanged glances; Kate didn't. She looked hard at me and said, "And they're on their way here right now?"

"I sure hope so," I said.

"So," Kate said, "I'll ask you again: they're here because?"

"They're running security for Senator Hawke," I wanted to add "among other things" but, knowing Kate as I did, I'd decided that in this particular case, less is more, so I didn't.

I was uncomfortable playing by someone else's rules. In this case Casey Wu's. She was out there doing the work, and here I was sitting on my ass waiting, something I never was very good at...

Well, that was about to change, because the doorbell rang and Jacque went to let them in; I followed her.

She opened the door and came face to face with Elona Jackson, who was half a foot taller than her, and she froze, something I'd never seen her do before.

"Um, hi," Jacque said, looking up at the imposing woman.

"Hi, yourself," Elona said, the corners of her mouth turned upward in a cute little smile as she stepped past Jacque, who couldn't take her eyes off the woman.

I think I mentioned that Jacque's gay, right? She was so mesmerized by the amazon that she paid no attention to Casey, or Donald, or the hardass I knew to be Simon Wilder but had never met.

"Glad you could make it," I held out my hand and said, "Simon..."

It was like putting my hand in a vice and turning the screw.

"Harry Starke, I take it," he said, then suddenly let go of my hand.

Jacque ushered them into the conference room, where I made the introductions. Coffee was offered and brought, and when everyone was seated around the table, Donald Rockford set his hard case on the table and unfastened the locks. Tim's eyes shined.

"Is that what I think it is?" he said.

Rockford responded positively, and what followed was an exchange regarding different models of rugged military computers with satellite capabilities and multichannel encryption that only they understood.

"By the way," Donald said, finally, "nice trick you pulled to get into my TSA servers. A little advice for the future, though, randomize access points and emulate interaction."

He winked, and while no one else understood what the hell that meant, Tim seemed to take it in like it was a piece of wisdom from the ancients. He looked like a kid at Christmas, getting instructed by his older brother on how to play with his new toys. He watched intently as Rockford connected his monstrous laptop to our flat screen on the wall and then ran through his slide presentation: TSA, Nero, and then Senator Andrew Hawke and his upcoming tour.

"So," Kate asked, when he'd finished talking, "what's the plan?"

"We need support and access," Wu answered. "First and foremost, we'll need priority access to every location on Senator Hawke's itinerary. Naturally, we'll provide our full cooperation, and whatever information we have with regard to the assassin, Nero, to your department, Sergeant."

Kate didn't answer. She was frowning.

What the hell's going on behind that pretty face, Kate?

"What do you need from me and my people, Agent Wu?" I asked.

"All of the above, Harry," she said, "and I do appreciate it."

She paused, then said, "Look, I know how outlandish all this must seem, but I promise you, we're not here to play spy games. My main concern is Nero. Once he is out of the picture, CPD can take over. We were hired to keep the senator safe, nothing more."

It was a load of crap, and I knew it. I'd heard it all before. It reminded me of the office politics I'd managed to escape back in 2008—one team pitching a plan to another, trying to get people on board, to share intel, to coordinate… It wasn't going to fly, not in my house, but I decided to play along, see where it took me.

"Sounds like a plan," I said. "Who's your contact in Senator Hawke's camp? We need to get in touch and figure out a plan. I… have a few ideas of my own." I didn't, but I would, when I needed them.

Wu said, "Hawke's head of security is Roger Booker."

Another familiar name from my father's past. If my memory served me right, Booker also attended the same high school as August, although he wasn't part of that elite club that went on to become career politicians. *Well, he ended up close enough, I suppose.*

"Great," I said. "Let's give him a call and invite him in for a chat. Now, it's time to get to work, people!" I looked at my watch. It was almost seven o'clock. "Forget that. Go home and get some sleep. We'll begin early in the morning."

9

The meeting was, for all intents and purposes, over and people began to leave until only Wu, Wilder, Bob, Kate and I were left. Wilder was whispering something to Wu I couldn't hear. Kate looked at me. She obviously had something on her mind, and I could tell she wanted to talk.

"What are you thinking?" I asked, in a low voice only she could hear.

"Can we talk in private?"

"Let's go to my office. You want more coffee?"

She shook her head.

"Casey?" I said, rising to my feet. "I need a few minutes with Kate, okay?"

"Sure. We'll wait."

I looked at Bob and nodded. He nodded back, but there was something about the look in his eyes that told me he wasn't happy.

My office had become my second home. It's huge, cozy, with a giant stone fireplace, bookshelves, a handcrafted walnut desk and, of course, the second love of my life—Kate being the first—my custom leather desk chair.

I flopped down onto one of the two sofas. Kate locked the door and sat opposite me on the other sofa, the coffee table between us.

I lay back, put my feet up on the table, and said, "What's bothering you, Kate?"

"I'm out of my depth, Harry. This is big. I think I need to bring the Chief in on it."

"It is big," I agreed. "Might be the biggest case we've ever worked."

"I'm glad you realize that, and I hope you also realize that I can't keep it under wraps for long. I have three bodies, a rogue security agency, and a possible assassination on my hands... not to mention your involvement."

I understood and even shared her concern. She wasn't worried that the case was too big for me; she was worried about the magnitude of the events that called for her—and the CPD's—involvement, which meant she'd need to take the case over at some point, possibly even force me off it. That's if Finkle allowed her to keep it, which because of its potential high profile, I doubted.

As if I'd let that happen.

"Relax," I said. "You go ahead and do what you've got to do, Kate, and I won't get in the way. But let's work together on it, what do you say?"

She nodded, smiled, and said, "You have a plan, then?"

"You know I do... Well, I'm working on one."

"Oh dear. That means you don't have a clue. You'd better get a grip, Harry," she said. "I have to report what I know to Finkle, and when I do, all hell will break loose."

Assistant Chief Henry Finkle was my former and

Kate's current boss. He's a hardass, an egotist, a misogynist, and a racist, and he has a tendency to overreact and come to the wrong conclusions. I could imagine him sticking his nose into every nook and cranny, causing chaos and confusion and generally screwing things up for everyone in his effort to find Nero and take the credit for himself. Maybe I'm exaggerating, but then again, maybe I'm not.

Either way, the CPD would be getting in our way. I had to think of something, and quick.

I said, "You're right, Kate, but think about it this way: Nero's already here, somewhere in the city at this very moment, planning his hit. If the cops put out an APB on him, it'll be all over the news. Senator Hawke will probably cancel his visit, and then Nero's gone! We'd be losing our shot at him. No pun intended."

Well, some pun intended, but that didn't matter, because Kate slowly nodded. She said, "I can give you twenty-four hours, Harry, but then I'm gonna need a rock-solid plan. Something I can pitch to Finkle without freaking him out."

"Done and done," I assured her, even as the gears in my head were already spinning.

"Thank you," she said, rising to her feet.

I walked her to my office door. We kissed, and I held her for a moment longer than a simple "thank-you" kiss required. I knew we had some hard days ahead of us, maybe even weeks, and I desperately wanted to hold on to the moment.

"What *are* you going to tell them?" I asked as she unlocked the door.

"That we have an addict on our hands, possibly ex-military, hunting down dealers."

"Maybe you could tell them he's some kind of vigilante?"

"I'll think of something," she said. "But you'd better get this right... Look, I have to go. Tonight? Your place or mine?"

"Mine. I'll cook steaks."

"Sounds wonderful," she said as she opened the door and, in one fluid and decisive motion, stepped out and left.

Me? I went to rejoin the others in the conference room. Wilder was absent.

"What's the word, Casey?" I asked as I sat down beside Bob. "Where's Wilder, by the way?"

"Simon's taking a bathroom break," she said. "I called Booker. He'll be here on Friday. His number two will handle the rest of the senator's tour until he gets to Chattanooga. We have less than a week to come up with something he'll believe and agree to."

"More than enough time," I said. "Listen, there's something I need to discuss with you."

The door opened, and Wilder stepped inside and sat down beside her.

"Your formal involvement?" Wu said, smiling. She brushed aside her hair. "I'm not new to the private sector, Harry. It's about money, right? But hey, I don't mind. Let's discuss it with Booker when he gets here, and I promise I'll convince him to hire you."

That, Agent Wu, I thought, *is not the answer I was looking for. It's not about money, not at all.* Out loud, I said, "Excellent."

"Nice to have you on the team, Harry," Wilder said.

There was something about the way he said it I didn't like, but...

"Likewise," I said. "Okay then. Are we done? If so, I need to get out of here."

We shook hands and then went out to the front office. The TSA team was ready to leave, and as they did, I saw Jacque miming a phone to Elona, mouthing *call me*.

"She seems... nice," I said to Bob as the door closed behind her, not really knowing what else to say.

Bob said, "Not my type."

"And you ain't hers, dummy," Jacque replied, playfully elbowing him in the side.

We laughed, then I went to call my father.

10

Two days later, I picked August up after his afternoon golf practice at the Country Club, and we headed for the airport.

I said, "Appreciate your help, August."

"I'll do what I can, Harry, you know that. I want to make sure Andy and Roger are safe. Not that they need my expertise here."

"Maybe not, but I have a feeling they're going to need mine. You're gonna be my backup."

He stared at me, his eyebrows raised, so I added, grinning, "Not in the field, Dad. I have a whole team for that."

My father had been supportive from the very beginning of my PI days, but he wasn't a fighter. August's strength was his mind, and it had served him well.

"Just how real is the threat?" he asked.

"That I don't know. I've been thinking about it over the last couple of days, and I'm not really sure if the murders are connected to the Senator or not. Nero hasn't shown himself since he took off in the van. Wait a minute... He jumped into the side door, that means... that... someone was driving. And that means Nero isn't a lone wolf at all. Damn! That puts an entirely different light on it."

We had just enough time to swing by the bagel shop and pick up coffee before Booker's plane was due in.

It was a little before ten when we arrived in the airport lounge. Casey Wu and Simon Wilder were already there, sitting together drinking coffee. I made the introductions and then listened as August asked them about the private security industry and the legal implications of their involvement in active combat situations. I couldn't tell whether he was purely curious, just idly passing the time, or testing them. If it was the latter, Casey Wu seemed to have passed it.

Booker's plane landed a few minutes later and taxied to the gate. We met him on the concourse where Casey attempted to make the introductions, but as soon as he spotted August, he was all smiles, and Wu became little more than the hired help. They hugged each other, as old friends do, and August introduced me.

Booker was a short man in his early sixties, with a silver goatee and a bald spot on top of his head, which reminded me of a Benedictine monk. His black suit looked expensive, but forgettable, and contrasted sharply with his white shirt and striped blue-and-gold tie. He carried a thin leather briefcase and was trailing an expensive-looking roll-on suitcase.

"Harry is a private investigator, Mr. Booker," Wu explained. "He's helping us track down Nero here in the city."

"Doing my best," I said.

August gave me a single pat on the back and said,

"Harry is being humble, Roger. He's a brilliant investigator."

"August, please," I said.

"Well," Booker said. "Casey speaks highly of you, Harry... May I call you Harry?"

"Of course, I—"

"Well," he interrupted me. "As I said, Casey is impressed, so we should talk. Casey?"

"We're meeting at Harry's offices in... well, thirty minutes, Harry?"

I nodded; Booker nodded. And with that, he seemed to put me out of his mind.

"It's been a long time, Roger," August said as he led the way down the steps and out to the parking lot.

Booker decided to ride with us to catch up on old times with August, but that didn't happen. August is a master interrogator and before we arrived at my offices, he knew more about Booker than Booker did. Booker laughed as he related the story he knew by heart: He, Booker, upon graduating from Washington and Lee University, had caught a ride to Washington, D.C., with their classmate Andy Hawke. Their impressive careers—politics for Hawke, security for Booker—had since then taken off.

Booker was excited to meet with his old friend, but I could tell he was tired, lacking enthusiasm. Not because of the trip, but because the long years of public service had taken their toll, and now his heart was no longer completely in it. How could I tell? Whenever August mentioned the Country Club or the exotic vacations he and Rose took, Booker perked up, was all ears, asking questions and saying, "That must be nice." No, the man was exhausted.

I know what you're thinking, and I agree. What the hell was this guy doing running security, for a senator, no less? No wonder he'd hired TSA to do the job for him. Casey Wu and her team had the energy, the know-how, and the resources necessary to do the job, and they worked outside the system, which meant they had a certain level of freedom Booker didn't have. I could relate.

We traveled I-75, past the Walmart parking lot on Greenway where Casey and her team had parked their trailer—I bet Rockford had something to do with getting the necessary permissions to park an 18-wheeler in the city—and then took the Germantown Road exit. From there to Georgia Avenue and we turned into my secure lot. I spent a few minutes talking with Jacque, and then I joined them all in the conference room.

"All right, ladies and gentlemen," Booker said, "let's get on with it. First, I need to know what the hell's going on here." He looked at Casey and then continued, "And I'll require a full written report for my file, Miss Wu."

"Understood, sir," she replied. "Donald will provide you with a copy. So..." and she proceeded to appraise Booker of the events of the previous several days.

She didn't pull any punches, which was good because he needed to understand the seriousness of the possible threat we were dealing with. Although Wu's team had been onto Nero for several years, this was the first time they'd had to deal with him directly, as an adversary. The fact that three people had already died seemed to shake Booker, and if he hadn't been too concerned before—there are always plenty of nutjobs in politics—he sure as hell was when Casey had finished her dissertation.

Wu closed her iPad and looked across the table at him, waiting for some sort of reaction, I presumed.

He sat for a moment, contemplating his notes, then looked up and said, "That's truly disturbing. I didn't realize the full weight of the situation. Has the local police force been notified? The sheriff's department?"

"Yes, sir," I said. "They are aware of the threat, and they've agreed to keep a lid on it until—"

"Keep a lid on it?" he barked. "They should be out there hunting this monster down!"

I was about to answer him, but Wu beat me to it: "With all due respect, Mr. Booker, Harry is right. We have Nero right where we want him, here in the city. We don't want to run him off... to fight another day, so to speak."

"I don't follow," Booker said.

Yes, you do, you old goat. I was sure he did. I was also sure he was more than a little overwhelmed.

"He is planning an assassination, Mr. Booker," I said. "We don't know who ordered it, but that's beside the point for now. Our best shot at stopping him is right here in Chattanooga."

Booker glared at me for a moment, and then he glanced at August, who had been listening quietly.

August looked across the table at him, leaned forward, put his hands together, and said, "Sounds like a catch-22 to me, Roger. You can delay the problem, but it's not going to go away. I agree with Harry and Miss Wu. You need to stop this maniac here and now."

Wu nodded. "Absolutely. If we spook him now, who knows where Nero will pop up next? Together, I believe we can nail him before he does any more damage."

Booker took a deep breath and sighed audibly. I almost felt sorry for the man; he was... trapped and, I think, in over his head. I felt even worse for Senator

Hawke: he was still out of the loop and didn't know a thing.

"What do you suggest, Casey?" Booker asked.

She opened her iPad, flipped through several screens, found what she was looking for, looked up at him and said, "Mr. Wilder and I have been analyzing Nero's patterns, and we have compiled a fairly comprehensive list of his potential—"

Booker cut her off, "That's irrelevant. I'm not hearing a solution, Miss Wu. If you're asking me to put the Senator's life in danger, you can forget it. I expect better from you than some damn list of... whatever. We know what... who the threat is. Now, what do we do about it?"

"If I may, sir?" I asked.

He turned his head, glared at me, then said, "Go ahead, Harry."

"I suggest we run a good old-fashioned sting operation."

11

A sting operation?

That got their attention. The room went silent. Ten pairs of eyes stared at me, puzzled, but eager to hear more. Then:

"No," Booker said.

Everyone turned away from me, looked at him, then back at me, then again at Booker. It was as if he and I were playing a very slow and weird game of tennis.

"So, let me see if I understand you," he said. "What you're proposing is that instead of taking all precautionary measures to make sure that Senator Hawke is not exposed to this maniac, we organize a special event and use him as bait? Did I get that right?"

"Yes and no," I replied, hiding a grin.

Any reaction was better than no reaction at that stage, and he was already brainstorming ideas, which was a positive. It would take some more convincing, but I knew my plan could work—if I could only figure out exactly what that plan was.

Once again, Wu lent me a hand, saying, "It might not be such a bad idea, sir."

Booker fiddled with his pen. I took it to be a nervous tic. He stared at his tablet, sucked on the pen, looked up at me, shook his head, sighed heavily, and said, "I'm listening, Starke, but you'd better make it good. I don't see Andrew going for anything that... Let's put it this way: he's all politician and no guts... Sorry, August."

I glanced at my father and saw him raise an eyebrow at Booker.

"I understand completely," I said. "What I'm suggesting is that we add an event to his schedule, a speech in some public place, someplace we can fully control."

"Like a university?" Booker asked, frowning.

"Too risky," I replied. I had considered such, but if there was one thing I wasn't prepared to deal with, it was hundreds of twenty-something students.

"Universities are too crowded," I said. "Too many young people and campus cops with little training. We need to do a little research."

"We'll make a list, sir," Wu said. "Harry and I will work on creating some options."

"I don't like it, Casey," Booker said, then looked at me. "What else do you have in mind, Harry?"

I stood, walked over to the window and looked out onto the street, thinking, taking my time, very well aware of the people seated around the table behind me, waiting.

"It has to be a public place," I said, "worthy of the Senator's attention. It has to be legit, because of the seemingly spontaneous change to the Senator's schedule. Is there anything already on his schedule that you can move up?"

Booker flipped through the screens on his tablet, took a notebook from his briefcase, opened his pen, jotted something down, and then said, "There are a couple of radio appearances, but I'd have to talk to Senator Hawke about those. Would either one of those work?"

"No... no," I said. "Too small We need to drop one of those and find something bigger, something with a live audience, lots of people..." I leaned back against the window, my hands on the sill beside me, my mind spinning.

"No colleges, universities, or schools," I said. "Forget radio and TV... Hmm..."

Rockford began typing on his laptop. He looked up at the monitor on the wall behind Booker. Everyone turned to look at it; Booker was the last to turn and stare up at it. He flushed with sudden anger, turned and said, "That's his schedule. How did you..."

The hacker grinned and said, "I'm nothing if not efficient, sir, but you did share the schedule with Casey, did you not?"

Booker glared at him, then at Wu, shook his head, frustrated, then turned in his seat to stare up at the screen.

"See anything, Harry?" Wu asked.

I'd been studying the schedule during Booker's exchange with Rockford, and I'd spotted a couple of possibilities. I pushed myself up off of the windowsill, stepped over to the big screen, pointed, and said, "Open up these two, Donald. Please."

I saw Wu nod out of the corner of my eye.

"I don't know, Starke," Booker said, shaking his head. "I don't feel comfortable with... improvisation."

He'd picked the wrong time to annoy me.

"Beats having Senator Hawke dead, doesn't it, Mr. Booker?" I snapped.

The reaction around the room was instant and palpable: I could have sliced the silence with a knife. I didn't give a shit. I was trying to keep Senator Hawke alive, and he didn't feel comfortable?

"Sir," I said, "this guy has already killed three times. He won't give up. It's better we take him on our terms rather than his, don't you agree?"

I was becoming more and more frustrated with Booker's lack of understanding and... enthusiasm, but his was the ultimate decision, so I had to keep him focused.

Meanwhile, people began excusing themselves, some for coffee, some for a bathroom break, and some, embarrassed, to leave altogether.

The first to leave was August.

"Thank you, Roger, Harry, everyone," he said, "for allowing me to sit in, but I'd better be on my way. Let's have dinner tonight, Roger, what do you say?"

"Of course, August. I'll call you... when I get done here," he said, dryly, glaring at me.

"Jacque," I said, "would you mind running August home for me, please?"

Tim made an excuse and left, and then Ronnie opted out of the meeting. I didn't mind; there was little for them to do since Rockford seemed to be happy handling the IT.

"Let me know if you need anything, Harry," Ronnie said.

"We could do with some coffee," I said.

"I'll ask Tim to do it," he said and closed the door behind him.

I turned back to the screen and said, "What do you think about this first option, Casey? AT&T Field."

"The baseball stadium? Could work," she said. "How do you picture it?"

"Senator Hawke will be giving a speech there before the game, correct?" I asked Booker.

He nodded. "Andrew's a big Lookouts fan, so yes, he'll make a speech there before the game, a week from today."

"Good," I said. "Can you bring up the map?"

It took Donald a single click, and the next moment we were looking at both the stadium's aerial map and detailed schematics of the approaches, exits, maintenance hallways, etc. The stadium was quite new, built in 1999 and named Bellsouth Park. The name was changed in 2007 when AT&T bought out Bellsouth. Unfortunately, it was an assassin's dream. Looking at the aerials and the schematics, there was no way to cover all of the possible vantage points without calling in the national guard.

"We could surround the Senator with bulletproof panels, like they do when Obama delivers a speech, and have our people scout out the surroundings..." Even as I was saying it, I realized what a monumental task that would be, especially considering the geography.

Finally, I said, "Nope. It's too complicated."

"How so?" Booker asked, alarmed.

"The space is too open. There is no way in hell we can canvass all that downtown area or possibly keep an eye on it during the event. You need to cancel that event, or at least postpone it until after we get the bastard..." I trailed off, thinking hard.

Wu nodded. "Agreed. Harry's right, sir. You should postpone the event."

He nodded and said, "He's not going to like it, not one bit."

"I'm sure he won't," I said. "But as I said, better that than dead. Next."

Rockford closed the window and opened up another one.

I stared at it for a moment, the excitement growing inside me, and said, "Now this... this is better. This could work."

The last item on Senator Hawke's tour of the city was a speech to the students at the Chattanooga Police Academy. It was the first class to be held in conjunction with the Tennessee Law Enforcement Training Academy at their brand-new facility located north of the city in Hamilton County.

"But that event is still a month away," Booker said.

"It is, which is why it's perfect. We need to reschedule it. We need for him to make his speech on opening day instead."

"I don't see how that's any better," Booker said.

I looked at Casey. She was smiling, looking at me knowingly, waiting for me to explain.

"But it is," I said, "for several reasons. First, and most obvious, the place will be packed with cops. Less obvious, but a key factor nonetheless, is that rescheduling the Senator's appearance will throw Nero off his game, give us the element of surprise."

"Go on."

"Just as we are making plans to keep Hawke safe, so Nero is out there somewhere planning to kill him. You've said he thinks five steps ahead, right?" I asked Wu.

"Nero likes to be prepared, yes."

"Exactly. The chances are, then, that he's already made plans A-through-Z for every one of the Senator's public appearances. We can't allow him the luxury of choosing from multiple venues. If we do, we're at a massive disadvantage. We have to make sure he has only one choice; we have to create a situation we can control."

"By moving up the event?" Booker said.

"Not just that: by staging the event and canceling the rest of his schedule—"

"What?" Booker yelled. "We can't do that. Hawke won't allow it."

"We can... We have to. He can reschedule after the event. The new Training Facility opens five days from now. That's more than enough time. It's perfect."

"How can we cancel his entire schedule and make it believable?" Booker asked. "Surely this man is smart enough to figure it out, that we're laying a trap for him."

I rubbed my chin. I had a plan in mind but didn't want to share it just yet.

"That's a good question, sir," I said, "and it needs a little thought. How about we meet again tomorrow? Same place, same time. I'll have a detailed plan for you then. And, Casey, I'll need your help."

She gave me one short and precise nod, the same motion I'd seen Bob and other ex-military colleagues of mine do. Everyone began gathering their belongings, except Booker, who was still playing with his pen, not convinced.

Wu said, "Sir?"

He frowned, and then put his pen away and produced a handkerchief, which he used to pat at his forehead and bald spot on his head. He said, "I must say, Harry, this is quite a departure for us... for me. Miss Wu, I expect you to keep me updated on your progress. I'll talk to the Senator and—"

"With all due respect, sir," Wu said, "I don't think

that would be wise. The fewer people that know about our plans, the better, at least for now. So far, it's just you, my team, and Mr. Starke's. We can't afford any leaks."

"I can vouch for my people, Mr. Booker," I said, "and I do agree with Miss Wu. Give us a couple of days to put it together, and if it still doesn't work for you, we'll... have to work with what we have."

I wasn't impressed with Booker. I could tell he wasn't persuaded but, finally, he closed his briefcase and prepared to leave. Casey volunteered to take him to his hotel. Me? I stayed where I was, sitting at the head of the table with Bob at my side.

"You didn't have much to say," I said when the last person to leave had closed the door. "What do you think?"

He leaned back in his chair, stared at me, frowning, then shook his head and said, "I think you're embarking on a very dangerous game, Harry. You could get the Senator killed..."

He let the pause hang for a long moment, but then his frown slowly morphed into a gleeful smile, and he said, "But I love it and I'm with you. I'm not sure about Booker, though."

I nodded and said, "Neither am I. He's a wild card, no doubt about it, but we have to live with him, at least for now... August thinks highly of him, and that's a plus, I suppose, but I think the man may be burned out, too long in the job. I dunno. I'll talk to August. In the meantime, we have a job to do, right?"

"That we do," he agreed. "You gonna talk to Kate?"

"Absolutely. We're going to need her help on this one."

~

It was after nine when I heard Kate's key in the front door lock.

"Harry, I need a drink," she said as she slipped out of her jacket and flung it onto a barstool. Her holster, Glock, badge and cell phone she unloaded onto the kitchen counter and shoved them as far away from her as she could. She was exhausted.

I had an open bottle of Riesling in the fridge. I poured her a glass. She grabbed it and downed it in one go, then held out her glass for more. I obliged.

She set it down on the counter untouched and said, "I'll be back." Then she headed to my bedroom.

I heard the shower running, and a few minutes later she reappeared wearing only one of my T-shirts. She'd untied her ponytail and let her blond hair fall to her shoulders. I gotta tell you, my heart skipped a beat.

"I need something to eat," she said, grabbing her glass. "Chinese?"

"Sounds good to me."

I grabbed my phone, called Dinner Delivered, and placed the order. I was told forty-five minutes. Easy! Sometimes technology can be a real asset.

We went to the living room to wait. The river was a sheet of silver and orange metal: not even the merest ripple broke the surface. Kate finished her wine and then snuggled up against my chest, dozing; life was indeed good, but I was still too wound up to enjoy it. I opened my iPad, went online, and began browsing through images of the new training facility.

The doorbell rang, and I eased myself out from under Kate and went to grab our delivery. When I returned, Kate had my iPad in hand.

"Sorry," she said, "you left it open. You don't mind, do you?"

I smiled, admiring her almost-naked body. She, however, looked up at me warily and said, "Why are you looking at pics of the new academy, Harry?"

"Give me a minute and I'll tell you," I said, setting the food down on the coffee table and beginning to unpack it.

While I worked, I filled her in on our meeting with Booker, including my idea for the sting operation. Kate listened without comment, just nodding from time to time as she ate. That is until I explained my idea for the Training Program speech, at which point she stopped eating and turned and stared at me.

"So, you want to invite Nero to take a shot at Hawke... at the freakin' police academy? Are you nuts?" she asked. "Oh... my... God!"

"In a controlled environment," I said defensively. "We'll have our teams on the ground. We'll dictate the narrative, Kate. Entry points, vantage points, everything."

"And you need me to talk to the Chief about it?" she said doubtfully.

"That'd help, for sure. We don't have much time, Kate, and we need to scout the location and coordinate with the PD. You're aware of the threat. You know who this guy is."

"What about the sheriff's department... and the State Police?"

"No, just the PD. It's your first class at the academy. He'll expect them to be there. If we include the sheriff and state, he'll know something's up and may call it off to play another day."

"Well, I don't know. I'll have to go directly to Johnston. It will be his call, and you know how he can be."

"That I do, but you need to talk to him ASAP. You want me to go with you?"

"No! I'll handle it... Oh, and by the way, I have some good news for you."

And she did. Lt. Mike Willis, head of CPD's CSI, had identified the bullets Nero was using. They were 6.5 Creedmoor, used for long-range competitive shooting and hunting, effective to and, in the right hands, beyond a thousand yards.

Why was this good news? Two reasons. First, the CPD knew they had a professional killer on their hands, which meant that Chief Johnston would at least listen to Kate. Second, it gave us a radius of his field of fire. No matter how good Nero might be, I was sure he would want to up his odds for success and stay well within the designated range. We had real numbers to work with. Now, it was up to Kate to trust in me and my idea.

She did.

"It sounds crazy, Harry," she admitted, "but it also sounds doable. There's gonna be some pushback from the higher-ups, but if Senator Hawke is all in, then I think we can convince the Chief to play along."

"Thank you," I said, and I kissed her, but I didn't have the cojones to tell her that Hawke didn't even know about the plan yet.

12

I'll spare you the tales of the office politics and the hoops Kate had to jump through to get it done. Suffice it to say we—that is me and Wu—could do nothing without the Chief's okay, so that next day was a real test of my patience.

It went pretty much as I expected. He called us both in, Wu and I, and Kate, as the lead detective led the pitch while Wu and I filled in the details, provided visual aids in the form of maps and schematics, as well as the arguments in support of the whole idea, but it wasn't enough. Johnston called Roger Booker to get his confirmation and to make sure that every effort was being made to protect the Senator. All of which he would have done a month later anyway when the speech at the Academy was originally scheduled.

Booker had already spoken to Hawke, and I was surprised to learn that he was wholly onboard and even excited. The man was, after all, the consummate politician, operating under the premise that any publicity was good publicity...

Even if it kills your silly ass? I wondered.

Only then, when he knew Senator Hawke had given his blessing, did Johnston give us the go-ahead to use the new facility and begin to make preparations.

"Better late than never," Kate said when we stepped out of his office.

"I guess. We'll have to wait and see."

Later that afternoon, Senator Hawke's office sent out press releases announcing that, for personal reasons, he was canceling his tour and that his speech at the academy would be the final event.

And so, with just three days left, Kate, Bob, Tim and I were in my Maxima heading north, followed by Wu and her team in a blacked-out Cadillac SUV.

The landscape changed—rolling fields, woodland, farms, tiny communities—and I was once again reminded of how beautiful East Tennessee was. Lost in thought, I drove on, wondering what the hell I'd gotten myself into; besieged with visions of what might go wrong, of Senator Hawke lying crumpled on the dais, his head split apart by a high-velocity bullet.

"Harry?" Kate said.

I heard her, but I didn't, if you know what I mean. I drove on, staring fixedly out through the windshield.

"*Harry!* Where are you? Are you okay?"

I turned my head, glanced at her and said, "I'm fine, just ruminating, is all." I didn't mention the visions. She was well aware of my supposed abilities.

"I was just thinking about the last couple of days: the stupidity of the bureaucracy... It's... It's like herding cats, trying to get anything done in a hurry. I'm so glad I'm not a part of it anymore."

"Oh, but you are," Bob said, "at least for this op."

"That's true enough," Kate said. "I know it's frustrating, but even the Chief has his superiors, and they all have to be brought in, give their approval."

"Sheesh, don't I know it... So much for secrecy. I'd be willing to bet Nero knows more about the plan than we do."

"Oh, come on, Harry," Bob said. "It's all about politics, you know that."

He was right, and I knew it, but that didn't make me any happier. I trusted my gut feelings more than I did anything or anyone else. *Too many,* I thought. Besides Senator Hawke, the Chief also had to bring in the Mayor. Not a problem. As soon as he learned about Hawke's plans, to not only speak at the Academy but to also be part of a sting to catch a killer, he jumped right in.

Oh yeah, it all sounded great on paper: our potential future governor—and maybe future president—delivers a speech, and in the process, Chattanooga's finest apprehend an international assassin! That would put a lot of feathers in a lot of caps, and that, of course, was the deciding factor. The mayor gave his approval, but I didn't believe he had any idea of the risks, and even if he did, he was prepared to take one hell of a gamble.

And again I had the vision, and I know I actually shook my head, but no one said a word.

"We'll need to work fast," Bob said. "But at least we have access, thanks to Kate."

It was true. As the only sworn officer among us, Kate had been given full access to the academy compound.

We'd done a lot of homework, though. Tim had hacked into the satellite system so we had access to the latest overheads of the site; thus we had an idea of the layout and, most importantly, the obvious vantage points Nero might go for. "Might" being the operative word, because not for a second did any of us expect him to do the obvious.

13

We turned off Highway 153 and drove for about a mile to the new facility. It was located on what once had been a poorly placed, eighteen-hole golf course. Its geography being its main problem and ultimate downfall. The course had been privately owned, cash-poor, and badly managed. Having said that, the layout itself wasn't too bad and lent itself admirably to its new role. The idea now was that the new complex would be used by law enforcement agencies for all of East Tennessee.

We parked in the large lot in front of the training center administrative building. Elona parked the Cadillac next to us and the TSA team stepped out of their vehicle. In their black jackets, jeans, and sunshades, they looked like a dangerous bunch and were missing only the comms in their ears to complete the look. I hid a smile as we crossed the lot.

"Charming place," Rockford said.

It was a typical government facility: a three-story building of red brick, yellowish-white cement blocks, and tinted glass; flagpoles out front, neatly trimmed bushes, and crude but lackluster flowerbeds set at equidistant intervals. On a slab next to the steps was a bronze plaque that read:

Tennessee Law Enforcement
Training Academy
Building A

We mounted the steps to the front doors and filed inside; I was the last to enter.

We were expected and were greeted in the lobby by an officer, identified by his tag as Officer Monahan, who checked us in and issued visitor passes.

Monahan was a tall, thin man with a friendly clean-shaven face and short, white hair. I'm sure I wasn't the only one that felt like a member of a tourist group visiting a museum.

"Gather round, everyone," Monahan said, "and welcome to the Tennessee Law Enforcement Training Academy. I am, as you already know, Officer James Monahan, and I'm now going to take you on a tour of the facility. Please follow me."

"We are in Building A," he said as he walked ahead of us, "which serves mainly as the administration building, but there are some classrooms and study rooms here, as well."

"How many?" Wu asked.

"Classrooms? Twelve, I think, and as many study rooms. I'd have to check with the Captain, though."

Wu nodded. I'm sure Rockford had already analyzed the layouts of every building in the complex, just as my team and I had done. Perhaps, Wu was testing Monahan, which wasn't such a bad idea. Had we had more time, I would've insisted on interviewing every officer who would be present on the day Hawke was to make his speech, testing them on their knowledge of the facility. We needed every available man and woman to be aware of their surroundings—because Nero wouldn't forgive any mistakes. It would be unforgivable if the Senator was killed because some rookie cop couldn't find an emergency exit.

Monahan completed the tour of Building A, and we exited through a pair of double doors at the rear that gave access to the main yard—a wide, spacious area that reminded me of my own stint at the academy many years ago. We stood on the steps for several minutes, talking together and studying the rest of the facility and the terrain beyond. While it all still had that boot camp feeling I remembered, it was a far cry from the academy I attended.

Some one hundred yards away to our right sat Building B—similar in design to A, but six stories high instead of three. It was flanked by Buildings C and D, both five-story barracks of red and yellow brick, with small square windows and outside stairs that reminded me of a low budget motel.

Directly ahead of us was the stadium—a soccer/football field encircled by a running track. Beyond that was the obligatory obstacle course and then, further out, six shooting ranges, each of which featured open shelters complete with tables and shooting rests. I surmised that the designers had, where possible, incorporated the wide, asphalt cart paths that once had been a part of the failed country club, and turned them into running trails. Indeed, I could see a formation of cadets jogging in the distance.

It was, however, the stadium and its surrounds I was most interested in. It was there on a small stage that Hawke would make his speech. That would be followed by a short concert by the police band.

The entire facility was surrounded by trees—forest—interwoven by a sprawling web of hiking trails and paths.

"Beautiful," Wu said, interrupting my thoughts.

"Indeed," I said.

And it really was. And everyone was nodding, except Rockford whom I assumed, like Tim, wasn't impressed by wide open spaces and the great outdoors.

"Isn't it?" Monahan said. "So, what would you like to visit first?"

"How about we split up?" I said, turning to Wu. "You guys have more experience with outdoor operations, so why don't you sweep the grounds and woodlands beyond the facility. My team will begin with Building B."

"I'm familiar with the facility, Officer," Kate said. "Why don't I show Mr. Starke's people around while you can take care of Agent Wu and her team?"

Monahan hesitated, then nodded and said, "Will do, Detective."

I checked my watch. It was just after ten o'clock.

"Let's rendezvous back here at two and exchange notes," I said.

"Sounds good," Wu said.

They mounted two golf carts and headed off toward the perimeter.

Building B was a facility unto itself. The ground floor housed a swimming pool, a gymnasium, several lecture halls, two conference rooms, a library, and a number of study rooms. We ignored all of those, instead focusing on the top four floors and the rooms that overlooked the stadium. They were all still vacant, still unassigned, dusty, quiet, echoey.

We stood together, the four of us, me, Kate, Bob and Tim, looking out of one of the top floor windows. *Oh yeah, I thought. I can imagine Nero hiding somewhere up here watching the opening ceremony. It's the perfect vantage point for a sniper: it's what? Maybe three hundred... three-twenty-five yards; he couldn't miss.*

"It's perfect," Bob said. "Easy-peasy for a pro like Nero."

"Yeah, and that's the problem," I said. "One, he *is* a pro, and two, he won't do the obvious; do what we expect him to do... This isn't it."

"I agree," Kate said. "Not because of what you said, but because getting out of here after making the shot wouldn't be easy. He'd have to make his way down six floors, and by then we'd have the building surrounded."

I nodded thoughtfully. It was indeed a perfect spot, perfect for us. While I was sure Nero would likely be elsewhere, always supposing he'd show up at all, we'd make sure by denying it to him. We'd put our own sniper up there, give him the best seat at the show.

"We can work with this," I said distractedly, but I didn't explain, not then.

We inspected a couple more rooms on the upper floors, and then we left Building B and went to check out the barracks: Buildings C and D. They too offered a good view of the stadium, but the chances of escape were even worse. Nero would either have to run down the five flights of outside stairs or take the emergency stairs inside the building. Neither one was a viable option. I just couldn't see it, so I discounted Buildings B, C, and D. Building A? It was impossible. There was no way he could even get inside that one... or was there?

Who the hell knows what the man is capable of?

So, with the buildings inside the complex discounted, we were left with the wooded area surrounding it as the probable location for our assassin. *Oof.*

We grabbed a golf cart and made a lap around the stadium, checked out the obstacle course and the ranges, and discounted them all.

We briefly crossed paths with Wu and her team near Building A. She paused, acknowledging us with a slight nod of her head and saying, "There's no need for you guys to do the surrounds. We got it. There's a lot of walking to be done down there, fellas, Kate. No access for carts."

"You think we can't handle it, Agent?" Kate said with a smile.

"Oh, I'm sure you can, but why bother?" she said, smiling back at her. Then she walked confidently past us, her team trailing along behind her. Elona carried Rockford's suitcase of a laptop, seemingly without effort, as he followed, trying not to fall behind, sweating and cursing.

Simon Wilder also seemed unaffected by the hike, but he wasn't smiling. I figured he must have been doing the same as I was: analyzing, planning, calculating. There was something about the man I couldn't get a handle on. I don't think he'd spoken more than a couple of dozen words since I'd met him.

"I think we should check out the surrounds for ourselves," Bob said as we watched Wu and her team enter Building A.

"That we should," I agreed. "That we should."

The wooded area—more wilderness than parkland—that surrounded the training complex was a sprawling web of innumerable, narrow woodland trails, each identified only by colored tags nailed to the trees. Time was short, but we needed to check it out. I decided the best way was to split up, each of us taking a path. I chose the River Trail marked with green tags and—alternately fast-walking and jogging—followed it all the way to the water, finding the experience both meditative and enjoyable.

I imagined Nero, having taken his shot and disassembled his weapon, jogging down this path with a twenty-pound duffel bag on his shoulders. He'd be running faster than I was, and he might even decide not to stay on the path, but to go where? When I reached the river, I knew it wasn't an option... unless he had an inflatable stashed somewhere close by.

I stood for a moment on the riverbank, listening to the sounds of nature. Thinking.

No, Nero wouldn't come this way. The opening ceremony is set to begin at noon. He'd have to cover the two miles on foot in broad daylight, with hundreds of cops on his ass; dogs too. It would be suicide, and Nero isn't a fanatic or a terrorist. He's a hired gun. To him, it's just another job, not a political statement. He'd plan his escape as meticulously as he would the hit.

I turned back, walking this time, and met Kate, Tim, and Bob at the obstacle course.

I let Tim catch his breath, then said, "I think the woods are a no-go. The only option for escape is the river, and I don't see it. It's too far, unless our friend can fly."

"Or go underwater," Tim said. "We know he's an expert diver, right?"

I hadn't thought of that. It would be easy enough to hide scuba gear out there... still...

I nodded and said, "That might work, but it's one hell of a hike to the river, and... No, I don't think so."

"So, where does that leave us?" Kate asked.

"I have a couple of ideas, but let's get back to Wu. We've done all the recon we have time for today, but we'll be back." I turned to Bob. "You need a hand there, old buddy?"

"Screw you..." he began, but then just shook his head as if he was disgusted at the idea: I knew better; Bob can take a joke.

A few minutes later, we reconvened with TSA outside Building A. With the exception of Rockford, they all looked like they'd just returned from a stroll in the park.

Wu said, "Seems pretty clear to me, Starke. What about you?"

I studied my reflection in her sunshades, then glanced at her people, and said, "Yes, seems clear enough to me too, but let's not talk here. Let's go back to the office."

"You have a plan?" Wu asked.

Oh, yeah, I have a plan, I thought. *And I have a feeling I'm not the only one.*

14

Officer Monahan, who'd been listening to the exchange, didn't say anything. Instead, he just shook his head, turned away, and walked up the steps into Building A.

Wu and her team waited for me to answer. My crew knew me well enough to realize that wasn't going to happen, not then anyway. The pause in the conversation became uncomfortable, but still nobody spoke.

What was I thinking about? To be honest, I was trying not to think at all. I needed more information, and the situation was stressful enough without my entertaining any loose, unsubstantiated thoughts, so I didn't.

It was Rockford who, too tired to participate in the theatrics, finally said, "Can we go, or what? I can barely feel my legs." And then he turned away and started up the steps after Monahan, who was waiting patiently at the doors, obviously unsure of what he should do next.

Wilder nodded, and he and Elona followed the hacker, and then so did Wu. Nothing was said by anyone as we followed Monahan through the building to the reception desk where we surrendered our passes, checked out, and then walked out onto the front steps and down to the parking lot. It was almost three o'clock.

Wu stopped to light a cigarette, puffed out a cloud of smoke, and stared at me, a slight, enigmatic smile on her lips.

"Meet you guys at the office," I said as I opened the car door and slid inside.

"We'll give you a head start," Wu called.

I waved a hand at her and closed the car door.

For maybe ten minutes as I drove, nobody said a word. Me? I was wondering if Rockford had bugged the Maxima. It wouldn't have surprised me if he had.

Finally, Kate couldn't hold it in any longer: "What the hell's going on, Harry?"

I continued to stare out of the windshield, not sure what to say. I opened my mouth to speak, but before I could Bob said, "He doesn't trust them, and rightfully so."

"Yeah," Kate said, "no shit. Then why are we meeting them at the office? Wait, are they even coming?"

"Oh, they're coming," I said.

"Oh, my God, Harry. I swear it's like pulling teeth to get anything out of you. Okay, I'll bite. Explain... like I'm five years old."

Bob, seated in the back, chuckled; I smiled, couldn't help it.

"I told you I have a plan, right?" I said.

"Yeah, a plan to protect the Senator. I know that; what I don't know is how you plan to do it, and how Wu's... squad comes into play?"

I considered laying it out for them there and then. But something told me they were better off not knowing what

I had in mind, which is why I was searching for an answer. I decided on a white lie... *Damn it!*

"I'm not sure myself," I said, "not until I talk to Wu, which is why I asked them to meet us at the office. For now, just know that they'll be taking part in the sting."

They all knew me well enough to hear and identify the BS, but unlike Bob and Tim, Kate had a little more at stake: she was the CPD's representative in this operation, an equal partner, so to speak.

"Give it up, Harry," she said tersely. "You can BS everybody else, but not me. You want me in, you talk to me... Now!"

I glanced sideways at her. Her face was set, determined. I gave in, nodded, and I shared my plan with them... Well, not quite.

Did I tell them the whole truth during that car ride? Perhaps, not... Ha, no, not at all, but at that moment, my gut, sixth sense, whatever, told me it was the right decision. And, as you know, I trust my gut in all things... Well, mostly, so I shared the plan I intended to share with TSA.

When I was done, they just sat there, silent, for several minutes. I was about to speak when Bob said, "I find it hard to believe, Harry."

"Which part?" I asked.

"The part where any of what you just told us makes sense, Harry."

I shrugged, grinned, and said, "You'll see."

15

On the way back from the training facility, I made sure to drive by TSA's mobile HQ parked at Walmart's lot on Greenway to make sure it was still there. It was, but their black Cadillac wasn't. We arrived at the office shortly after four o'clock that afternoon.

Tim went directly to his cave. Jacque was already in the office, ostensibly holding down the fort, and she made coffee for everyone and ordered pizza. Ronnie, it being a Saturday, was playing golf at the country club. Bob and Kate took their coffee and went to the conference room.

Me? I stepped into my private office, telling them, "Be with you in a minute. I have to call August."

Another white lie.

My office is my retreat, a place where I go to think, my go-to when I need peace and quiet. It was also the only place in the complex, other than Tim's cave, I knew to be secure. I'd had Tim install one of his gadgets; a device that was constantly sweeping the room for bugs and would ping my phone if such a device was found.

I took out my iPhone and called Tim. Yes, I know he was just two doors away, but I didn't want anyone to know I was talking to him. In the car, I had given my team the part of my plan that they needed to know. And now, I gave Tim a piece of the puzzle specific to him. Sometimes I think the boy knows me better than I know myself. I heard him chuckle as I told him what I needed.

Wu and the others arrived shortly after I finished the call, and we all gathered in the conference room, everyone except Elona, that is. She'd hung back to make coffee for herself, an excuse to chat for a moment with Jacque. I swear she'd shared more words with my office manager than she had with any of us since I'd first met her in that trailer.

The car ride must've refreshed us, because there was no tension in the room when I entered. Rockford was on his laptop, headphones on, as he manipulated different maps and schematics of the training center on the flat screen monitor on the wall. I sat down, and we watched as he quickly constructed a simplified map of the academy compound and its surrounds that included every trail, path, building, and exit. In another life, Rockford might have been an artist.

"Mr. Starke?" Roger Booker's voice boomed out of the conference call speaker on the table. He was in Memphis.

"I'm here, Mr. Booker."

"That's everyone, then," he said. "Please proceed."

"Why don't you take it away, Casey," I said.

Wu and Wilder glanced at me, and then Wu nodded and signaled for him to speak. He got up and walked over to the screen.

His map of the compound was graphic, but simple. At the bottom was the parking lot in front of Building A.

Above it were Buildings B-through-D. Together, they formed the eastern side of the rectangular complex. The northern and western perimeters were bounded by dense forest. In the center of the complex, parallel to Building A, was the stadium, above which, to the north, were the obstacle course and the shooting ranges.

Wilder pointed to an area of the forest at the top left of the map. "The terrain here and here," he said, "is covered with dense woodlands interwoven with numerous hiking trails, some of which lead all the way to the river, here." He pointed.

I glanced at Bob and smiled, hoping no one else noticed.

"I know Westwood," Wilder continued. "He's a sniper, yes, but he's also a survivor." He pointed to the stadium. "The stage is located here, facing Building A. We all agree that Building B would be the perfect vantage point for a sniper, but escape from there would be almost impossible, right? And, due to their orientation, there's no direct line of fire from either Building C or D, agreed?"

Everyone nodded agreement.

"That leaves just two possibilities: Building A gives him a straight line of fire at a hundred and twenty-five yards." He pointed to it and, with his finger, drew an imaginary line to the stage. "But once again, Nero would find himself in a difficult position and almost certain to be captured, or killed, so that's out."

Wilder turned away from the screen and looked in the direction of the conference table, then continued, "That leaves him only one other position that offers a clear line of fire to the stage... here." He pointed to an area of the forest close to the top of the map, beyond the shooting range and the obstacle course. "It's a shot of about five hundred yards. No problem for Westwood. He'll likely use a hunter's shooting stand in one of the trees to give him the elevation he needs for a clear shot."

I nodded, taking it all in.

Wu stood and joined Wilder at the monitor. "So, Harry, we'll place Simon on the top floor of Building B, here. We, that is my team, will sweep the woods to the north. Your team can take the forest to the west."

It was exactly what I figured they'd want to do. Strategically, it wasn't the worst plan I'd ever heard. You cover all your bases, have snipers watching from above, and unless Nero's a magician, you'll get him.

Still, I said, "I like the sound of that. We can cover more ground by cutting off the sections we know for sure he isn't going to be. Bob and I will be on the ground here." I pointed at the western woods. "And, yes, you can cover the area to the north. Kate, you'll be in the stadium, on the stage with the Senator, in case Nero decides to get up close and personal. I think we're all set."

There was silence as we waited for Booker to announce his final verdict.

He said, "For the record, I am still not happy about the position we are putting ourselves into." He paused, and then added, "Senator Hawke is on board. He's had his press secretary announce that he's canceled his tour, pleading exhaustion and the need for rest, and that the event at the Academy will be his last. Not literally, I hope," he said dryly.

"We're flying into Chattanooga the night before the event, on Monday," Booker continued. "I know that's cutting it close, but it can't be helped."

"Thank you, Mr. Booker," I said. "We'll be ready for you. Please, give our regards to Senator Hawke."

Booker muttered something unintelligible and hung up.

We spent the next several hours discussing and redrafting Wu's plan. I let her take the lead, rarely intervening or arguing, observing her and her team. It was the first time we'd actually worked together, a rare opportunity for me to gain some insight into the way her mind worked, and how TSA operated as a unit.

By the end of the night, when everyone was thoroughly tired, we had a pretty good idea of how the big day would go. We were certain Nero would show up—he no longer had a choice—and we thought we knew where. We also thought we knew how to stop him.

By eight-thirty that evening, we'd all had enough. We'd worked the plan to death; there was little more we could do. It was now all up to Nero. Would he play by our rules? I doubted it.

16

The next day, Sunday, we were all back at the training facility, ostensibly to do a final sweep of the area and consolidate the plan. The stage had been fully erected, and the staff was setting up the seating: three hundred chairs in three equal sections. Rain was not in the forecast.

It must have been sometime around noon when I found myself standing on the running track that encircled the stadium. To my right were the two barracks buildings, C and D. The forest was to my left, beyond the ranges. Building B was slightly behind me and to my right.

Will it work? I thought. *I sure as hell hope so, because if it doesn't... Well... that doesn't bear thinking about. But if my gut's right...* I shrugged. *If it's not, if I'm wrong, Senator Hawke's a dead duck, and I might as well be too. Damn! What have I gotten myself into?*

On Monday evening, Casey Wu and I drove to the airport to meet Booker, Senator Hawke, and his wife, MaryAnne.

"This thing with Nero," I said to Wu, as I turned into the short-term lot. "It's personal... for both of you, isn't it?"

She thought for a minute, then nodded and said, "I suppose on some level, it is. I always thought Albert was my friend. And he was, until... well, you already know what happened."

"He must be angry," I said, "that you didn't join him when he needed you. Maybe he thinks you betrayed him... and perhaps you did."

Why was I baiting her this late in the game? Maybe I wanted to put her off-balance, maybe I was simply becoming impatient with the enigmatic Asian.

"Maybe I did," she said, staring out through the windshield. "Who knows? I haven't seen him in years. As I said, he's a ghost. Come on," she said, opening the car door. "Let's go meet the Senator." And she stepped out and walked away.

Hmm, maybe I tickled a nerve.

The Senator arrived a half-hour later to little fanfare, just a half-dozen journalists from the local newspaper and TV stations. We had to wait while he talked to them, which gave me an opportunity to observe the man.

Andrew Hawke was of average height, lively, animated, in his mid-sixties with perfectly coiffed silver hair and a smile that lit up the entire concourse. I watched with interest as he performed for the cameras. He was good, and the hacks loved him.

His wife, MaryAnne, was fifteen years younger, a platinum blond. She'd been Miss Tennessee a couple of decades earlier. At fifty, she was still stunning. Her light blue eyes sparkled, especially when she smiled, which she did a lot. She waved, shook hands, took questions; it was hard to tell who enjoyed the attention more, she or her husband. They were indeed a lovely couple, and it was easy to imagine them in the Governor's mansion, or even the White House.

Finally, the small crowd thinned, and they made their way toward us, Roger Booker leading the way, three security guards around the Hawkes. I stepped forward to greet them.

"Pleasure to meet you, Harry," Hawke said. "I've heard good things about you."

MaryAnne also extended her hand and said, "A pleasure indeed, Mr. Starke."

17

MaryAnne Hawke was not just beautiful, she was probably the most approachable woman of her status that I'd ever met. Instead of taking the SUV with Booker, Wu and her husband, she elected to ride with me in the Maxima.

"You sure, honey?" Hawke asked her.

"Why, of course. Mr. Starke is keeping us safe, Andy. Unless you mind?" she asked me.

I shook my head. "Not at all. But I have to warn you, my ride might not be what you and the Senator are used to." I offered a slightly embarrassed smile, but she only shook her head and smiled back at me.

As we followed the SUV back to the city, MaryAnne looked sideways at me and said, "You're wrong, you know."

"Wrong? About what?"

"This car. It's fabulous. The seats could use a deep clean, but the ride is smooth as butter... You've modified the engine, haven't you? Jazzed it up a little? Added a couple horses?"

I chuckled. "That I have, Mrs. Hawke."

"Oh, my Lord. Please don't do that. How about I call you Harry... and you call me MaryAnne? "

"If you insist," I said, smiling at her.

"I do."

"You have a good ear, MaryAnne," I said, and the car rumbled when I stepped on the gas.

"My father had a sixty-eight GTO when I was a child. That was back in Knoxville. He was an absolute fanatic, dragged me along whenever he went to his garage to tinker with it. It was his idea of entertaining us kids. I know a hot motor when I hear one."

"A Pontiac GTO, huh?" I said. "An amazing muscle car. Worth a fortune today."

She nodded and began to talk about her childhood; and she talked, and she talked, and by the time we reached the safe house, I'd begun to feel as if I knew more about her than did her husband... and maybe I did. I was also beginning to think that she was hitting on me... well, flirting a little anyway, and maybe she was. Then again, maybe it was no more than the years of working politics alongside her husband. Whatever it was, MaryAnne Hawke had the talent to captivate. Hell, truth be told, I didn't want the ride to end. But it did, and I reluctantly dropped her off and turned her over to her security team.

Having seen her safely inside the house, I took a few minutes for a quick chat with Wu and Booker about the events planned for the next day, then I left them to it and went home.

I poured myself a goodly measure of Laphroaig and took it out onto the patio, to think. These were indeed momentous times.

By eleven that night I was in bed, alone, but sleep

didn't come easily. The beast that lives in the dark corners of my bedroom came to visit... an omen? Perhaps. Eventually, I drifted away, with thoughts of MaryAnne Hawke lingering...

18

"I hope you had a good night's sleep?" I asked Tim the next morning.

"I didn't sleep much, to be honest," he said. "Tried to write an algorithm and it didn't work. Not yet, but it will, eventually."

"I believe you," I said. "We're meeting Kate, Bob, and the TSA team at the training facility. We'll go in my car."

I helped him load his equipment into the back of the Maxima.

His laptop wasn't military grade like Donald's, but neither was it a standard piece. He'd upgraded and enhanced it to a point where the manufacturer wouldn't recognize it.

"You know the plan, Tim. What do you need me to do?"

"I'm not sure we'll have the time to do anything, Harry. I'd need access to their system, and Donald keeps it well-guarded."

"Didn't he show you their trailer?"

"Yeah, but he had Cover OS on."

I glanced at him, puzzled. Tim explained: "You know how, when you go to a Best Buy, they'll have phones and laptops with a demo slideshow playing? Basically, Cover OS is just that—a complex screensaver made to look like a working operating system."

I nodded slowly. It was important that I kept tabs on Wu's team, and I knew, from what Tim had just told me, that was going to be problematic. So, to some extent, I'd have to trust them, but I'd also have to trust my instincts.

"Do what you can, Tim. I need intel."

We turned into the academy lot shortly before nine that Tuesday morning. Wu's eighteen-wheeler was already there, parked conspicuously across a dozen spaces on the west side of the lot.

Officer Monahan met us at the entrance; we had specifically requested for him to be on shift. The man was visibly nervous, but also excited.

"They're waiting for you outside, Mr. Starke. I mean, on the other outside."

"I've got it, officer," I said, smiling. "How are you feeling?"

"Nervous. Hoping for the best. You know? It's a big day."

"That it is," I agreed.

Wu and her team were waiting for us inside Building A, in the reception area. They were dressed from head to toe in black combat gear complete with shades, holsters and, with the exception of Wilder, they were carrying M-4 assault rifles. Wilder, though similarly dressed, was carrying an aluminum gun case and had a duffel bag over his shoulder.

"You wanna go over the plan again?" I said.

"If you think it's necessary," Wu replied.

I did.

By the time we were done, we were an hour out, but I still had a couple of things to take care of, but only after everyone had dispersed.

While our teams had coordinated our movements with both Booker's main security team and the Academy's own police forces, we still operated as independent agents and so were able to move around freely.

The presentation was due to begin at noon. We still had a little time. I took Bob and Tim back inside Building A for some instructions of my own.

Rockford had supplied our comms, much to Tim's displeasure. The TSA earpieces worked when you tapped on them, but both Tim and I had a feeling they were always listening, so I left them with Officer Monahan while we talked.

"What are you up to, Harry?" Bob asked.

"You know me, Bob. You know what I'm up to."

He frowned but didn't say anything. "What do I need to know?"

"I just want you to be careful and expect the unexpected," I said.

"How unexpected?" he asked.

Tim glanced nervously back and forth between us. He wasn't a field agent, so I could imagine his anxiety, but the kid was handling it well.

"I'm thinking that all is not as it seems," I said, "that we can expect a major snafu, so be damned careful out there, okay?"

Bob shook his head. "Shit! I knew it!" he growled. Then he took out his phone, inserted an earphone, and dialed my number. "Stay on the line, Harry. Keep me updated."

"No need for that," Tim said, grinning, as he set his aluminum case down and opened it.

"Here, use these." He handed us each a tiny earbud and a small wireless communicator. "I have one for Kate, too. I'll be listening in."

I slapped him on the shoulder and said, "You never let me down, do you? Thanks Tim. What about their comms? Can you monitor their movements?"

"I'll do my best," he said, nodding. "Umm, but you'll need to use theirs, right? If you don't, they'll know somethings up. Harry... we're treating them as if they're the enemy?"

"Right," I said, "and maybe they are, or maybe I'm just being paranoid. But don't worry, Tim. I'll keep you apprised of what's happening."

Tim nodded and said, "Give me a few minutes then. Let me see what I can do." And then he disappeared into a vacant study room to set up his laptop.

Bob and I went outside to get in position, Rockford's comms in one ear, Tim's in the other. I hoped to hell the chatter wouldn't be distracting. Just to be on the safe side, I removed the TSA comm unit from ear. I didn't want them overhearing my conversations with Bob.

As Bob and I walked together, I explained my plan to him... well, some of it.

"Geez, Harry, that's a hell of a gamble. How sure are you?"

"Not too sure at all, but Kate will be with Hawke, along with half the cops in the county, so I'm not too worried."

That was a lie. I was petrified, had to be. Fear is a primal instinct, essential for survival; without it we'd all be dead. I replaced the TSA comm unit in my ear.

So, as I stood on the steps of Building A, looking out at the stadium straight ahead, Bob went to assume his position in the forest to the west. Me? I took a deep breath and reminded myself that I was supposed to be good at this—and know what the hell I was doing. Hah, if only!

Twenty minutes later I tapped Rockford's earpiece and said, "Everyone in position?"

"Yup," Bob said.

"Will be there in a few," Wu said. Her position was in the woods north of the stadium, at the top of the map, so to speak.

"Elona and I are here," Kate said. They were at the stadium, waiting for Booker, Hawke, and MaryAnne.

"I'm in position," Wilder said from the top floor of Building B.

My other earpiece buzzed and Tim said, "I can hear you all loud and clear. And, Harry, I'm into Rockford's system."

"Roger that," I said. "Everyone stay alert. I'm beginning my sweep."

The assumption, so everyone had agreed the previous evening, was that Nero would be somewhere in the forest either to the north or the west.

The plan that everyone had then agreed on was that Bob and Wu, along with a couple of dozen cops and four of Booker's security people, would cover the perimeter of the forested areas. Wilder, in a top floor room of Building B, along with a PD SWAT team positioned on the roof of the building, was tasked with keeping watch over the entire complex. Kate and Elona would be on stage to protect Hawke, should something go wrong. Me? I was the free agent, roaming wherever I deemed necessary. We did, in fact, have the entire complex under surveillance... Well, I had to believe we did.

It was a good plan, under the circumstances and given the timeframe involved, which was tight. I planned to follow it... Not. Of course not.

The idea, so everyone thought, was for me to head out into the field and work in a clockwise direction, checking in with Bob first. Except, I knew Bob could handle things without me.

By eleven forty-five, the stadium was filled, and the many officials involved in the establishment of the new facility were giving their speeches; Senator Hawke would be introduced at noon.

19

I tapped my TSA earpiece and lied, "I'm on my way, Bob."

"Copy," he replied.

Instead, I moved toward Building B, hoping that Wilder would be too preoccupied to notice. I snuck around behind the building, removed my TSA earpiece, stuffed it into my back pocket, and started up the narrow stairway to the top floor.

"Bob," I whispered, using Tim's comms, "how are things looking?" No answer. "Bob." *Damn it,* I thought savagely. *Maybe I've lost the signal inside the building.*

I ran up the six flights of stairs and arrived on the top floor, breathing hard. *Geez, I didn't realize I was that out of shape.*

Hoping the comms would work now, I tried to get Bob again: still no answer.

Damn it! What the hell's gone wrong?

Exasperated, I put the TSA earpiece back in my ear and heard Wu say, "In position."

I considered trying to raise Bob on the TSA comms,

but decided against it. The crowd had started applauding, and I knew it was time for Senator Andrew Hawke's speech.

I dashed into an empty room and looked out the window just in time to see the Senator walk onto the stage. *Showtime.* I ran out into the corridor and began walking door to door, opening them as I went. I was about three doors down, about to open door four, when I heard it—a loud explosion.

I opened the door, ran into the empty room and looked out the window. The sheds at the north end of the obstacle course were exploding one after the other, sending clouds of black smoke up into the air.

Shit, shit, shit...

I turned from the window, ran back out into the corridor, and took off running, my Smith & Wesson in my hand. Wilder, I knew, was posted as lookout in the room at the far west end of the building. I reached the door, stopped, listened, my ear to the door, and heard the sound of a cartridge being chambered in a bolt-action rifle. I tried to open the door. It was locked.

I took two steps back—that was all there was room for —and then threw myself at the door. It burst open, and I staggered headlong into the room: Wilder was at the window, rifle at his shoulder, sighting through the scope.

"Don't even think about it, asshole!" I shouted. Startled, he half-turned.

And then the world ended... or so it seemed. It took me several seconds to process what happened next. Wilder, ignoring me, turned again to his scope. No sooner had he done so than he was flung bodily through the air— blood spatter flying in all directions—and landed flat on his back, on the floor, dead. I didn't need to check. I could see the hole in his chest. The bullet had slammed through his tunic, body armor, and heart.

"Freakin' hell!" I yelled involuntarily, taken completely by surprise. "What the hell?"

I ducked low, approached the open window, and peeked above the sill. It was total chaos in the stadium six floors below. I ducked down, turned around, sat down, my back against the wall beside the window, and I stared, at first unseeing, at Wilder's rifle now lying on the floor beside his still body.

Outside, I could hear people shouting and screaming. I turned over onto my knees and again risked a peek out of the open window. The crowd had scattered, running this way and that, like a bunch of scared ants. The obstacle course and the shooting range were covered in a fog of thick black smoke.

On the stage, I could see Hawke and MaryAnne, surrounded by security. Kate was slightly to one side, her back to MaryAnne. And then I saw Elona Jackson turn and aim her gun at the Senator.

"Kate!" I shouted, not knowing if she could hear me or not with all the confusion going on around her.

She didn't, but it didn't matter; Kate had spotted Elona. She swung around, pointed her gun at Elona, and shouted something I couldn't hear, momentarily distracting her. Kate fired twice: the tall woman staggered back a couple of steps, folded, and fell to her knees, still trying to bring her weapon to bear on the Senator. Kate kicked the gun out of her hands, and Elona keeled over sideways, a pool of blood expanding rapidly around her body.

Hawke's security detail rushed him off the stage. I stood, stepped away from the window, and turned again to look at what was left of Simon Wilder. Funny thing is, I didn't feel a thing: not sympathy, sorrow, nothing. I just shook my head, left the room, and ran back down the hallway to the stairs and then down them three steps at a time. I was met at the bottom by Monahan and two police officers, all white-faced, guns drawn, and in dire need of direction.

"There's a body on the top floor," I said as I ran past them. "Seal it off and call for backup."

Outside, all was in chaos. People were running in every direction, trying to get away from the stadium, now almost covered in a thick pall of black smoke.

"Bob! Kate!" I yelled into my TSA comm unit. "What's the situation? Talk to me." But the unit was dead.

"Tim!" I shouted. "Can you hear me?"

"I got ya, Harry? I don't know what's happening... Everyone's GPS signal puts them right where they should be, except for you. What's going on? Where are you going?"

Both were good questions to which I had no answers. I had to stop, close my eyes, focus. I knew I was facing the stadium, though I couldn't see it for the smoke. I figured Wu was somewhere beyond the smoke screen, hundreds of yards away to my right. Kate had to be on the stage, no doubt trying to take care of the wounded... No, probably dead Elona. Tim was still in Building A, out of harm's way, I hoped, and Rockford should still be in the TSA trailer...

Bob?

"Bob, come in!" I tried the comms again. "Talk to me for God's sake," I shouted as I started across the compound through the smoke. I had no thought for the

Senator. I knew there were plenty of people to take care of him and MaryAnne. My concern was for Bob.

"Wu?" I shouted, tapping the TSA comm unit: nothing. *Damn it, damn it, damn it.*

And then I remembered Nero. *Where the hell is he?* I wondered. There was no telling where he was; probably long gone, if he had any sense, which I was sure he did. It didn't matter though, there was nothing I could do about him, not then anyway.

"Tim," I said. "You there? Where's Bob? I can't raise him."

"I can't either, but his GPS puts him in position. He hasn't moved since he got there."

I started to run, gun in hand, toward Bob's last known position.

"Keep going, Harry," Tim said. "You're almost there."

And that's when I saw him, seated on the ground, propped against a tree, eyes closed, a knife in his shoulder, just below the collarbone, a dark red stain on his chest.

20

"Bob!" I shouted as I ran to him, only taking my eyes off him for a moment to check my surroundings.

There were people moving around maybe a hundred feet away. I could hear them talking but not what they were saying. Their voices were muffled by the sound of the blood roaring in my ears. I stuffed my handgun back into its holster and fell to one knee next to him, not daring to touch him. He was breathing, but weakly. His face was white, his eyes closed.

I inspected the knife. It was a small balisong, or butterfly knife, the kind you see kids—and small-time hoods—play with, do tricks with. Its grip was made up of two halves that fold to hide the blade. That blade was stuck deep into my friend's chest. From what I could see of it, it was a slim blade, no thicker than my pinkie finger; not that it made a whole lot of difference... Bob was in bad shape.

"Tim, if you're there, send a medic to my location, now!"

Tim replied something, but I didn't really hear it over my concern for Bob. I simply took it for granted that help was on the way.

"Hey, Bob, stay with me, buddy," I muttered, more to myself than to him.

He took a sharper breath, then grunted, and opened his eyes, tried to smile, coughed, then closed his eyes again.

"Don't move," I said. "Help is on the way."

"Don't touch the knife," he said, barely above a whisper. "You pull it out, I bleed to death in under ten seconds. That bastard Nero is a pro." He coughed again.

No blood, thank God.

"I know, I know. Now shut the hell up, Ryan; save your energy."

I put a hand on his forearm and squeezed gently. *Where the hell is that medic?*

"You listening, guys? Bob is down. I'm with him, but he's in a bad way. Awaiting paramedics. Starke out." No answer. *Damn it!*

The medics arrived ten minutes later. Boy, was I ever pissed. They apologized, tried to explain about the chaos at the stadium, but I wasn't in any mood to listen. Helplessly, I stood back and watched as they carefully loaded him onto a stretcher, placed an oxygen mask over his face, and then carried him out of the woods onto a cart path and from there to a waiting ambulance.

Along the way I ran into a uniformed police captain. He was standing with his back to me, talking into his radio. I tapped him on the shoulder. He turned, startled.

"Wh-at? Who the hell are you?"

"Harry Starke," I said, flipping my temporary ID at him, "Senator Hawke's security. You need to search the area. The shooter is still out there somewhere. He stabbed my partner," I said, waving a hand toward the ambulance, which was already moving, its sirens blaring. "And radio the damn TWRA and the Coast Guard. He's likely heading for the river."

I didn't wait for an answer. I turned and ran toward the main complex, leaving the police captain standing there, staring after me, talking animatedly into his radio.

The area around the stadium had been cleared; the stage taped off and surrounded by a half-dozen uniforms. Three more ambulances were standing by. Three EMTs were on the stage gathered around what I assumed was Elona Jackson's body. Kate was nowhere to be seen. Dozens of cops were combing Buildings C and D. Building B had been cordoned off completely: no one was being allowed in or out.

Suddenly, Kate appeared, seemingly out of nowhere.

"Tim told me Bob's been stabbed," she said, her voice panicky. "How is he?"

"He's gonna be okay," I said, hoping to hell that he was.

"What the hell happened, Harry?"

"I'm about to find out," I replied, tapping my TSA comms unit. "Wu, are you there? Rockford?" Nothing.

Then, in my other ear, Tim said, "I'm on my way to find out what's happened to Donald, but Agent Wu is still in her position, at least that's what her GPS is telling me."

Like hell she is!

"No, Tim. You stay the hell away from Rockford until we know what we're dealing with. You understand? Answer me, damn it." But he didn't, he was already gone, and I was fuming. *I'll kill him. I'll freakin' kill him.* Tim, not Rockford, not yet anyway.

I turned to Kate. "What happened on the stage? I saw you shoot Elona... Wait, you know what, right now I don't give a damn. You'll tell me later. I'm going after Wu."

And I took off running, without waiting for her reply, north toward the forest where I knew Wu was supposed to be. I ran past the stadium through the obstacle course, now clear of the smoke, past the still-smoking remains of the sheds, and into the forest.

My goal was to find Agent Casey Wu, if that was her real name, but I had a feeling she was long gone.

I tried calling her as I ran. The concern in my voice was real, not for her safety, but because I figured she might be waiting for me, waiting to take me out. I didn't really think she was, but at that point I didn't know what to think. Two members of her team had just tried to kill the Senator. Had Nero somehow gotten to Wilder and Elona and convinced them to join his team? Was Wu a part of it? I hoped not. Did I trust her? Hell no, but I'd been wrong before... and I knew I couldn't underestimate Nero.

"Stay put," Wu shouted over the comm.

I came to an abrupt stop, breathing hard.

"Wu? Is that you? Where are you?"

My earpiece crackled with static, and then she said, "I'm here, Starke."

"You okay?" I was moving again, speed-walking in her direction along the narrow strip between the edge of the woods and the vague edge of the smoke screen.

"A little banged up, but I'll live."

"Stay where you are. I'll be right there."

I found her squatting under a tree wearing nothing but her black pants and her bra. Her signature black leather jacket was lying on the ground next to her. She'd taken off her white top and was holding it to her forehead; it was stained red with blood.

"Good to see you, Harry," she said, obviously unembarrassed by her lack of clothing.

I gave her a hand and helped her to her feet. "What happened?"

She took the top away from her head to reveal a nasty-looking cut to her temple. "The explosion... It took me by surprise and I fell out of the tree," she said ruefully, looking up into the branches, gingerly touching the cut with her finger. "I feel like such a frickin' idiot. It's not like it's the first time I've been under fire... Oh hell, Harry, you know what I mean."

She shook out the top, looked at it, shook her head and crumpled it up into a wad, then reached for her jacket, put it on, and zipped it up.

I stared at her, not entirely convinced, and said, "So, what the hell happened?"

"A diversion, probably," she replied. "We should have expected him to pull something like it." She looked up at me, unblinking, and in a low voice said, "Did he get him, the Senator?"

"No," I said, and I looked away.

"Whew, thank God. Did Simon get him?"

"No. Nero got Wilder."

"Oh no... No... *NO!* How? What happened, Harry?" and then she began to curse.

I opened my mouth to tell her about Elona, but then thought better of it. I decided to save that until later; her reaction to the news of Elona's death would be... interesting, useful even.

"We should head back," I said instead. "We need to get that cut seen to."

She nodded dejectedly, and I led the way out of the forest.

Kate was waiting for us when we arrived back at the stadium, and she wasn't pleased to see Wu. Her face was white with anger. I'd never seen her that way before.

"You piece of shit!" She stepped forward, fists raised.

I stepped between them, cutting her off.

"Take it easy, Kate," I said quietly. "Casey's hurt too."

"She doesn't look hurt enough to me," Kate snapped.

Wu stood behind me, her hands raised slightly in a defensive posture, and said, "Why don't you tell me what happened, Detective Gazzara, and I'll try to help. I'll answer any questions you have for me."

"I ought to arrest you right here and right now!" Kate snapped.

The cops around us seemed taken aback by Kate's explosion, but they didn't intervene. Several of them grinned, then turned away. They had more to worry about than a catfight.

"Kate," I said firmly, giving her a look that was supposed to tell her *I've got this*, then I turned again to Wu.

"Elona Jackson made an attempt on the Senator's life. She's dead."

Her mouth dropped open. She froze. Then she slowly shook her head and said, "That can't be right, Harry. Why would she? I've known Ellie for years—"

"Ellie!" Kate scoffed. "Why don't *you* tell us why she'd do it? For all we know, you gave her the order!"

Wu looked past me at her and said, "Then what am I still doing here?"

"I don't know, covering your ass, maybe?"

"Tim, you there?" I said.

"Yeah, I'm here," he replied right away. "I was listening. Didn't want to interrupt. I'm with Donald, in his trailer. We're trying to figure out what happened."

"Damn it, Tim. Did I not tell you to stay away from... Oh, what the hell. Stay where you are. We'll be there in a minute."

The two women, who'd put their argument on pause to listen to me, were now waiting for an explanation.

"Tim's with Rockford," I said. "Look, you two, how about we put our differences aside and try to figure this thing out, huh?"

"I can't leave the academy until this mess is sorted out," Kate said.

Wu nodded and said, "I need to get this cut treated first."

I looked at her. The wound was bleeding again, but she showed no discomfort.

"Officer Stacy," Kate said. "Please have one of the paramedics take a look at Miss Wu's wound."

Stacy, a tall guy in his mid-twenties, nodded, motioned for Wu to accompany him, and said, "Follow me, please, Miss Wu." She did and, with the exception of Kate, everyone else left too, leaving us alone together.

It was at that moment I had a thought... a thought that made my blood run cold.

"Hey, you've zoned out again," Kate said. "What's on your mind, Harry?"

She was right. I had. I was replaying the day's events in my head, trying to establish a timeline.

"She told me to... stay put," I said, barely above a whisper.

"Wu? When was that?"

I barely heard her.

"No, she didn't," I said, almost to myself. "What she said was, 'stay put...' I thought she meant for me to be careful around the fire, but she wasn't talking to me... Shit."

"What are you talking about?" Kate said.

But I stepped aside, my hand raised for silence as I spoke into the earpiece.

"Tim?"

"What's up, Harry?"

"Get out of there, n—"

"Oh, hey, Casey—" I heard him say, then nothing.

"Tim!" I shouted, but it was too late. I turned to Kate. "Let's go!"

And without waiting I ran up the steps into the rear of Building A, sprinted along the corridor, and out through the front doors, with Kate close on my heels.

"Wu!" I shouted from the top of the steps. No answer. The TSA trailer was still there, its ramp lowered, smoke rising from its vertical exhaust pipes. At least, that's what it looked like.

I scanned the lot, searching for a woman in a black leather jacket among the surging crowds. Nothing. She was nowhere to be found. A ghost.

"I don't see her," Kate said. "Do you?"

"No, but... geez! C'mon."

The smoke issuing from the semi had turned from gray to black and doubled in volume, and I could tell it wasn't coming from its exhaust pipes.

I ran down the steps four or five at a time, sprinted across the lot to the trailer, and ran up the ramp to find Tim in there alone, on the floor unconscious, a gash on the side of his head, bleeding.

Rockford's computers and most of the rest of his

equipment were on fire. I scooped my young buddy up off the floor, turned with him in my arms, and ran down the ramp, out into the open air—with only seconds to spare before TSA's mobile HQ exploded, throwing us both several feet through the air, to land on my back, on the hood of a nearby car.

Fortunately for Tim, though not so much for my back, my body took most of the impact. Slight as he was, his weight slammed into my gut, knocking the wind out of me.

I lay on my back on the hood of the car, gasping for breath, Tim on top of me, my head swimming, floaties before my eyes.

I sat up, hanging onto Tim, and checked his vital signs. He was breathing, but his pulse was hectic. The kid felt small and fragile, but he was alive. I watched as the trailer burned. *Too close, damn it. I need to get Tim to safety...*

But I didn't. Kate was there, her back shielding me, us, from the heat. So were a half-dozen uniforms. One of them took Tim from me and rushed him away. Kate held my arm as I slid off the hood of the car, and together, we ran.

Again, we got away just in time: the tractor unit, now completely engulfed in flames, exploded, and again I was hurled violently forward to land flat on my face on the asphalt surface of the parking lot.

I rolled over and looked around for Kate. She was on her back, several yards away, coughing her lungs up. I counted six burning cars in close proximity to what was left of the semi and trailer. Of Tim and the officer, there was no sign. I could only hope they'd made it safely away to the ambulances.

"Stay still, please, sir," a voice off to my left said.

"I'm fine," I said to the paramedic. "The kid? How is he?" I asked weakly. "Leave me alone," I said, stiff-arming him. "I told you, I'm fine."

But I wasn't. I tried to stand, but I couldn't breathe without coughing violently.

They helped me to my feet. They wanted to put me on a stretcher, but I was having none of that. With one on either side supporting me, they took me to one of the ambulances, gave me oxygen and a shot of something. Ten minutes later, feeling strangely ebullient—*what the hell was that shot?*—I turned to Kate, who was sitting beside me, and started to laugh at her.

"You... look like hell," I said.

"Huh? Are you serious? You need to take a look in the mirror."

"Where's Tim?" I asked.

"He's okay. They took him away a few minutes ago... Hey, hey, calm down. He's doing fine. They just want to keep him overnight, for observation."

I coughed, stretched, winced, and then figured I was good to go again until later when my back would stiffen and become one huge bruise.

I stood, walked a few steps, then turned and sat down again.

"I think I've figured it out, Kate," I said. "The whole damn mess. Well, most of it."

"Give us some space, please," Kate said to the paramedic.

He nodded and left us alone.

"Talk to me," she said.

I stood up, unsteadily at first, then began to pace back and forth in front of her, limping, trying to put my thoughts in order, and then to put them into words. It was as if I had a movie playing in my head; now I needed to lay it out for her.

"There was something wrong about the whole deal. I could feel it... you know how I get sometimes? Sure you do, but I couldn't figure out what it was that was bothering me; certainly nothing I could go to Booker with, or even you. But see, it was *their* plan, right? I mean, they laid it all out, our positions, Nero's possible locations, and so on.

"I had an idea it was all bullshit, but I played along, hoping to figure it out before the Senator's speech. Then, something told me Wilder was a plant. I almost reached him in time, but..." My thoughts were interrupted by a coughing fit.

I put a hand to my face, thinking. My head was pounding, my thoughts scrambling again.

"Nero killed Wilder, then?" Kate asked.

"Yeah, Kate. He did. I think it was actually Wu and her team Nero was after. He never intended to kill the Senator. It was Wu's team that was hired to kill Senator Hawke."

"So Nero got Wilder," Kate said, nodding, "and the rest of the team then went to Plan B. Elona Jackson went for the kill, but Nero blew up the sheds, as a diversion?" she asked.

"Yes," I said, "but not for us... for Wu."

She shook her head and said, "You're losing me."

"Okay, this is what I think happened. Bob went to the western part of the forest, right? Wu sent him there, remember? She guessed that's where Nero would be, and he was: he took Bob out."

Kate tilted her head, thinking. "But if it was Wu's

hit... what was Nero doing here? And why would he try to kill Bob?"

That's one hell of a good question, and I don't have an answer to it, not yet. But he's an assassin... a pro. Nah... Yes... Maybe. But why would he do that? He must have known that Bob was on his side... Yeah, but Bob didn't know, and knowing Bob...

"I don't know, not for sure, not yet... If it wasn't for him stabbing Bob, I'd have said he's one of the good guys... My plan, to have the Senator cancel his tour in favor of this one venue, did Nero a big favor. Just as we planned, it narrowed the options for the hit down to one. Wu, she didn't give a damn. If we hadn't done it the way we did, she'd have picked her venue from any one of a dozen. Somehow, though, Nero knew Wu had been hired to make the hit. Those guys and gals all know each other's methods, so, just as TSA knew where to expect Nero, he knew where to look for them."

"Like Wilder's spot in Building B?" Kate asked. "Where he planned to shoot the Senator?"

"Ah!" I shook a finger at her. "No, no, no! It's getting clearer. Wilder wasn't there for Hawke. He was there to kill Nero, but Nero was faster." I paused, thinking.

"There never was a Plan B, Kate. Elona was the primary shooter, had to be. She was within a few feet of the Senator. Why risk a long shot when you can do it up close and personal? Fortunately, she was distracted by the explosions and Nero's shot, giving you the chance to take her out. Good job, by the way."

"Wow, how the hell did you managed to figure it all out?"

I shrugged. "It's what I do. Do you see what I'm saying, though? Everything happened within just a few seconds, but Nero outsmarted them, us. All of us. The bastard sure knows how to prepare."

"Oh dear, Harry. I have so many questions."

"I know, but—"

"No buts, Harry. If I have questions, you can imagine how many everyone else will have: Chief Johnston, Senator Hawke, Booker." She sighed and shook her head. "Oh Lord, what a mess."

I grinned at her. "Ain't life a blast?"

"So, where's Nero?" she asked. "And where the hell is Wu and her computer guy?"

"We'll find out soon enough," I replied, getting angry as I remembered what had happened to Bob and Tim. "Two of my team are injured, almost died—Wu left Tim for dead—and I'm pissed, Kate. I'm going after Wu *and* Nero. But first, we need to have a chat with Roger Booker."

21

"What a cluster..." Booker stopped himself, kicking back in his chair at the head of the conference table. He took out a handkerchief and wiped his glasses, only smudging them further, then gave up and set them back on his nose.

Kate and I sat on either side of him. Ronnie and Jacque were at the hospital with Tim and Bob; both were now in stable condition.

Two of Booker's men were posted just outside the door, with three more inside the building and two more outside. We'd just finished explaining the situation as we thought it was, and Senator Hawke's chief of security wasn't happy, not one bit.

Neither am I. Tough!

It was late. Kate and I had spent the afternoon at the CPD being debriefed. After that, Booker had joined us at my offices where we were trying to make sense of what had happened. The only bright spot being that Senator Hawke was still alive... pissed, but still alive.

After I was done sharing my thoughts, Booker asked, "So that's your theory?"

"About Nero and Wu?" I asked. "Yes, until we catch them, it is. It's all conjecture, sure, but it's all we can come up with. Albert Westwood, AKA Nero, has a personal vendetta against his former squadmates. Somehow he knew they'd been hired to kill the Senator, and that's a mystery all its own. Who the hell hired Wu, and how did Nero find out about it? Again, we'll not get answers to those questions until we catch him, or Wu. But we have to know, because whoever it was that hired Wu is still out there, and there's nothing to stop him from trying again. One good thing, if there is such a thing, is that Nero managed to take out half of Wu's team. With Kate's help, of course."

Booker glanced at Kate. "Detective?"

"I agree with Harry. Someone hired Wu, and Nero found out about it and decided to screw her over. An act of revenge? Who knows?"

Booker nodded. "We've started our own internal investigation, independent of the Chattanooga Police Force—"

"About that, Mr. Booker," I said, interrupting him. "How did you come to hire Casey Wu and TSA?"

The man turned his head to me so fast I feared he'd snap his neck.

He frowned, and said, "Just what the hell are you implying, Starke? I should remind you that this operation, this... so-called sting, was all your idea?"

"I'm well aware of that, sir, thank you, but I believe it's a legitimate question. As is... where are Senator Hawke and his wife right now?"

Booker adjusted his glasses, then glanced at Kate, who

maintained eye contact with him. I knew I was playing a dangerous game with the man, but what the hell? What was the worst that could happen? We'd already failed spectacularly, so now we had to regroup, get to the bottom of what had happened, and how it had been allowed to happen, and then make sure it didn't happen again. And if I had to make enemies in high places, well... it wouldn't be the first time, and it sure as hell wouldn't be the last.

Booker might have had people outside the conference room, but at that moment he was on his own; two against one. He stared at me for a long moment, then sighed and said, "Andrew and MaryAnne are at a secret, secure location."

Secret, secure location? I thought, unbelieving of what he'd just said. *How freakin' cliché, and how stupidly nonsensical.*

It was one of those phrases that meant absolutely nothing. Think about it this way: two can keep a secret, if one of them is dead, right? That location was about as secret and secure as the local McDonald's. What I mean is: someone chose the location, someone else coordinated and cleared it with the higher-ups, said higher-ups are now privy to the information. A special team took the Hawkes to said secret, secure location, and another team was watching them, probably several teams working in shifts. My point is that, far from being secret and secure, its location was known to at least a couple of dozen individuals, and any one of them could have been a mole, and it only takes one. Scary stuff, right?

Kate said, "Are you sure it's safe?"

Before Booker could answer, I did so for him, "Of course it's not. Mr. Booker, I need that address."

"That is strictly against protocol," he replied, folding

his arms. "And why the hell would I trust you with it anyway, after the monumental screw up this afternoon? Only Detective Gazzara's quick thinking saved us from disaster."

He looked at her and nodded. She ignored him.

"You're right," I said. "Our plan at the stadium failed, but it didn't fail completely. We fended off the attack, and we learned who our true enemies are. I'd say that's a win... of sorts. But trying to hide Hawke isn't going to work. It's just an invitation for Wu to finish the job. You *can't* hide him... How many people besides you know where they are, ten, twenty, more?"

I caught the look on his face and nodded.

"That's what I thought," I said. "You've turned him into a sitting duck."

Booker reached down to the floor and grabbed his briefcase. "I think we're done here, Mr. Starke."

"Like hell we are," I said. "Kate, could you give us a moment?"

"Sure thing," she said, never breaking eye contact with Booker.

Kate stood and walked out of the room, closing the door behind her. Booker set his briefcase down again, and all was quiet except the barely audible buzz of the overhead lights.

"Okay, Roger, I'll be straight with you. I messed up today, and I know you want nothing more to do with me. To you I'm just some hotshot asshole playing detective, and that may very well be so."

I paused and stared at him.

"Go on," Booker said, quietly.

"You know I'm right about what we've learned today. You also know that I'm not your enemy, and that

I almost lost two of my own people today. So, let me make you a deal. Give me the address of your safehouse, just me, no one else, and I'll do my damnedest to bring Wu and her hacker boy to justice. Help me help you, Roger."

Booker considered it, tensing his lips and studying my face. "Do I know those things, Mr. Starke? The official investigation has barely begun, and we haven't ruled anything or anyone out yet. How do I know you're not in bed with Wu?"

"You know I'm not, because I was up there when Wilder was killed. I could've easily picked up that rifle and finished the job. Besides, I didn't even know you were coming to town until Nero began his killing streak... those three junkies, except..." And then it hit me.

"Except?" he asked.

"Except, I don't think Nero killed any of those people. I believe, if you search what's left of TSA's trailer, you'll find traces of Adderall. Same goes for Simon Wilder's body. We know that there were two men that night at Hammerhead's office, and I'm betting they were Wilder and Rockford."

"Hmm," he said noncommittally.

"So?" I said. "We're losing time. What's it to be, Roger?"

I had to believe he was smarter than he was stubborn, and he was. After a minute's hesitation, he told me the address, and then looked around, as if checking the room for spies hiding in a corner.

"I appreciate your trust, Roger."

"I'll let my people know you're coming."

We shook hands, and then I stood up to leave. I wasn't lying when I said we were losing time. I was convinced that Senator Hawke was in very real danger, if he was even still alive.

We exited the conference room together and came face to face with Kate.

"Good night, Detective," Booker said, "and thank you for what you did today." He shook her hand and left.

"What did you talk about?" Kate asked, knowing full well I wouldn't tell her.

"He told me to go screw myself... not in so many words, but..."

"Is that so?"

"Well, maybe it was the other way around, who's to say? Anyway, I gotta run, Kate."

She touched my hand and said, "See you tonight?"

I kissed her. "Of course."

"Be careful, Harry, whatever it is you're up to. Let me know if you need backup."

"I will."

22

By the time I got to my car, Booker and his entourage were already gone, and I sincerely hoped we weren't going in the same direction.

I punched the gas pedal, hoping that Chattanooga's finest were too busy to bother about a speeding Maxima.

But what was driving me? Duty? Yes. Anger? No. Oh yes, I was angry: angry at Casey Wu, but much more so at myself for not acting on my earlier suspicions, feelings. My gut had warned me and I'd ignored it. I'd had numerous opportunities to nail their whole damn team... *Tipton Security Agency*. I actually laughed out loud and banged on the steering wheel.

But that was all irrelevant now. My gut was talking to me again, and it was telling me it wasn't over; not yet.

It was after eleven when I arrived at the address that night, and I couldn't believe my eyes. It was a freaking mobile home park. The "secret secure safehouse" was a double-wide—three bedrooms, two baths, the works—but about as secure as a paper bag.

A trailer park on the edge of town. It wasn't exactly

the sort of place where you'd expect to find a United States senator, which is probably why Booker had chosen it. *Damn fool!*

As far as I could tell, the location had only two things going for it: it was isolated and it was fenced. *Sheesh, I've seen more attractive abandoned scrapyards. What the hell was he thinking?*

I considered parking outside the wire fence and sneaking in under the cover of darkness but decided against it. If I needed to take off in a hurry, it was better to keep the car close by. So, I entered the park through the open gates, past a black SUV that I assumed was occupied by Booker's security detail, and drove slowly down the main strip to the safehouse.

I had to shake my head in disbelief at the beat-up Ford pickup rotting out front next to a somewhat less beat up '90s sedan and... the obligatory black SUV. *That's the ticket. Nothing says "here we are" better than a government-issued monstrosity.*

I turned my car around and backed in next to it.

A curtain moved inside the trailer. A dark figure checked me out through the blinds. I left the car unlocked and stepped out into the night. A dog was barking somewhere in the distance, and I could hear music playing, but most of the trailers were dark. Only a row of dim streetlights illuminated the central strip of the park.

I stepped up to knock on the door.

I didn't recognize the guard who opened the door, but he seemed to know who I was.

"Evening, Senator, Mrs. Hawke," I said.

The Senator and his wife were seated together on a couch.

"Mr. Starke," Hawke said. "Welcome. It's good to see

a friendly face. No offense, gentlemen," he said to the two guards now seated at the kitchen table.

If they'd taken offense, neither of them showed it.

"Is this it?" I asked the two guards. "Just the two of you?"

They looked at each other, then at me, and then one of them said, "Mr. Booker said he didn't want to draw attention, that two of us would be enough."

Booker said that? I thought. *I'm beginning to think that maybe Bob was right. I need to take a closer look at Mr. Booker.*

"Then I suggest one of you move that hulking Cadillac around back and out of sight."

Again, they looked at each other. Then the one that spoke to me nodded, rose to his feet, and went to do as I suggested.

"Did we lose anyone today?" Hawke asked, somberly.

"Two of my people are in the hospital, but they'll be okay."

"Roger told us two people were killed," MaryAnne said. "That woman... who was on stage with us?"

I nodded and said, "I'm afraid so. It now appears that Agent Wu and her team were hired to kill you, sir, not the so-called assassin they called Nero."

"I see. What a cluster—"

"Andrew!" MaryAnne said sharply, cutting him off.

I had to smile, despite the weight of the situation.

"I intend to spend the night here, sir," I said. "I'll sleep in my car, of course."

"Nonsense!" Hawke said. "This is a pull-out couch, I believe."

"Can I make you tea... coffee?" MaryAnne asked, as the door opened and the guard returned.

"Coffee would be nice," I said. "May I use the bathroom?"

Hawke pointed with his hand, and I went to wash my face and hands.

That done, I stepped back into the living room. The two guards were on their feet and headed toward the door, about to exit.

"I think I heard something outside," one of them said. "Get back."

I did. I took a step back into the hallway and drew my weapon.

The guard pulled the door open and...

The muted stutter of a suppressed M4 assault rifle was unmistakable, like someone was operating a jackhammer underwater.

The guard staggered backward as a hail of bullets tore first into his body and then, as he fell, into the guy behind him. They both hit the floor together.

"Get down," I shouted at Hawke.

His reaction was instantaneous. He dived to the floor. MaryAnne, still in the kitchen, took cover behind the refrigerator.

"Stay exactly where you are," Casey Wu shouted as she slowly climbed the steps into the trailer, a pistol in each hand.

"Harry," she said.

"Casey," I replied, pointing my own gun at her.

"Put it away, Harry," she said, one pistol pointed at Hawke, the other at me. "Don't make it harder than it needs to be. Let me do my job. If you interfere, well, Donald is outside with an M4."

"That's not going to happen," I said mildly, my gun rock steady, pointed at her forehead. "You do understand that, right?"

"In that case, none of us will walk out of here alive. Just ask these guys." She motioned at the dead guards with one of her pistols. "Mrs. Hawke, come here."

"Stay put, MaryAnne," I ordered, but the woman was too scared. She took a step toward Wu, and then another.

"Good girl," she said, grabbing MaryAnne's arm and jerking her around in front of her. "Now, Harry, you have a hostage situation. Senator, it's your choice. Your life for your wife's. Tick-tock."

She was right, and she was holding all the cards. I could kill her—at twelve feet it was an easy shot—but then we'd all be dead within seconds. Unless... I decided to go for it. I put my finger on the trigger, feeling the pressure in more ways than one. I hate Mexican stand-offs.

"Whoa... Think what you're doing, Harry," Wu said.

But then, outside, the crack of a rifle, and a single shot ripped through the night outside. There was a thud, then a clank as something metal hit the ground.

Nero! I thought. That son of a bitch was right on time.

At the sound of the shot, Wu half-turned her head and glanced outside, but she didn't flinch.

"Good job, Harry. Smart thinking, teaming up with Nero."

I hadn't. Of course I hadn't, but I didn't try to convince her otherwise.

"Give it up, Casey," I said. "You're out of options."

"Oh, I don't think so," she said and smiled nastily as she put a pistol to MaryAnne's head. "Here's what's going to happen. We, MaryAnne and I, are going to leave you boys and take a ride. Now, we're going to step outside. If you make a move, I'll kill her and take my chances with

Nero. You, Harry, will shut the door behind us and lock it. Understand?"

"Do as she says, Mr. Starke," Hawke said. He was staring at Wu, the hatred in his eyes plain to see.

Wu smiled at him, nodded, and began to back out of the door, her arm around MaryAnne, pulling her tight against her body.

Would Nero risk it and take the shot? I hoped not. A 6.5 Creedmoor full metal jacket would tear through both of them. Any attempt to take Wu down would almost certainly result in MaryAnne's death.

Together, the two women stepped backward down the steps into the night, MaryAnne weeping softly, the gun against her right ear. I listened, expecting to hear a shot. It never came. I stepped to the door, closed it and locked it, but kept my hand on the lock.

I heard a car door slam shut and I opened the door again, just in time to see Wu speed away, engine roaring, tires squealing.

I looked around the trailer park. All was quiet. What few homes that had had lights on were dark now, the residents obviously wanting none of it. Only the single row of streetlights illuminated the road. I stepped outside, down the steps, then stopped dead. On the path, standing over Rockford's body and an M4, I saw a black silhouette, a rifle over a shoulder.

Albert Westwood stared at me, his cold eyes glittering in the dim tungsten light.

23

Hawke ran out of the trailer after me, spotted Nero, tried to stop, then slipped and fell down beside me, where he stayed, on his ass, still, like a possum, staring at the assassin.

The dim orange lights turned Nero's face—blackened with camo paint—into a mask any kid would have been proud to wear for Halloween. Nero didn't move, just stood there, studying us.

I pulled my weapon from its holster and aimed it at him.

"Stay down, Senator," I said, my gun aimed at the center of the killer's chest. Nero was maybe thirty feet away from me. At that distance I could've put five bullets in him in three seconds... had he not been wearing body armor, an easy stop for a nine-millimeter slug. Head shots are tough, especially in the dark. I hoped he wouldn't test me.

Nero didn't flinch. He showed no reaction at all. He wore what looked like a Glock 17 on his hip, along with pouches containing three extra mags, but he made no attempt to reach for it, nor did he attempt to bring his rifle to bear.

For several seconds we stood there, staring at each other, then Nero shrugged and stepped over Rockford's dead body.

"Right there is close enough," I ordered, but the assassin ignored me and continued his measured approach.

I realized his footsteps made no sound at all, which made the whole scene unnerving. My finger tightened on the trigger.

"Last warning, Nero."

He froze. A confused smile appeared on his mask of a face.

"Well, I never," he said with a smile. "Is that what they're calling me these days?"

The British accent momentarily threw me off. He sounded a little like Jason Statham...

"The name's Albert," he said amiably. "Al, if you fancy." And again he started forward, effortlessly, soundless, his rifle still over his shoulder.

"Last warning, Albert," I said, my gun tracking his chest.

Senator Hawke stood and scuttered back toward the trailer. Me? Unnerved by the assassin's confidence, I too took a step back.

Nero continued his approach, then stopped, less than two feet away from the muzzle of my Smith and Wesson.

"Tut, tut, Harry old son. If you're gonna shoot me, aim for the head. I'm wearing three layers of Kevlar."

He tapped his chest with one hand, while the other still held onto the strap of the rifle on his shoulder.

Again, I wondered why nobody from the surrounding

trailers was getting curious or calling the cops. Maybe they had, or maybe this was one of those neighborhoods where everyone minded their own business, even at midnight, even when machine guns and sniper rifles crackled in their back yards. Or maybe...

"We're all alone, here, Harry," Albert completed my thought. "What few people there are, are busy minding their own business, so please, feel free to try and blow my brains out, which, let's be frank, shall we? You don't stand a chance of doing."

"What do you want?" I asked, my gun still pointed at his chest.

"Same thing you do, Harry old fruit. And you, Andrew," he looked at the Senator, now half-sitting on the trailer's tiny stoop.

"Me?" Hawke said.

"Casey Wu. I want to find her, and I want to kill her."

There was little emotion in his words. He was simply stating the facts, with the same ease one might talk about the flavor of a particular ice cream.

"Then our goals differ, Albert," I said, "because I want to take her in alive."

"Bullshit," he replied. "That's what you have to do, but it's not what you want. How about we go inside and discuss our options like civilized people?"

I glanced at the body on the path behind him, and Hawke said, "I'd rather not go back in there."

Albert glanced inside the trailer, at the two dead security agents on the floor. He said, "That's a crying shame. Sorry I couldn't make it here sooner, but I am a wanted man, as you know. Fine. Let's stay outside then. I'm sweating like a bloody pig, anyway. I'd really appreciate it if you'd lower your gun now, Harry."

I didn't want to, but my arms were getting stiff, especially my right hand. *Screw it!*

I holstered the weapon, half-expecting the assassin to jump me, but he didn't move.

"Thank you. Now, Harry, before we begin, let me apologize for what happened with your partner."

I glared, taking deeper breaths, seriously considering taking the gun back out and shooting the bastard.

He said, "Bob's a good bloke, and he fought like a lion, but I couldn't let him get in the way. Hope you can understand that."

Oh, I understood, all right. I understood that when all was said and done, I'd put a knife in Albert, just to show him how it feels...

"No hard feelings?" Albert said, pushing the hood of his tactical suit off the back of his head.

"Oh, a whole bunch of hard feelings, *Al*."

"Fair enough. In my defense, Senator Hawke is alive, isn't he?"

Hawke got up to his feet and shut the trailer door. He said, "What are you talking about?"

With Albert filling in some details, I proceeded to explain to the Senator what had happened at the training facility that afternoon. There was no getting around the facts: Albert Westwood had stopped Casey Wu's attempt on Hawke's life, and he was the one who took care of Simon Wilder. Kate and I helped, but I'd been sloppy with TSA, and the Senator had almost paid for it with his life.

When we were done, Hawke said, "Oh Lord, then I owe you both my life."

Albert and I exchanged glances, and he grinned.

"You're very welcome, Senator. Just doing our job, right, Harry?"

"That we are," I agreed begrudgingly. "By the way, how did you escape from the forest?"

Before replying, Albert took off his rifle and set it on the roof of the beat-up sedan. "My shoulder's killing me. To answer your question, I hid up a tree and waited for everybody to clear out. Hence my tardiness."

It sounded plausible enough. Special ops were skilled in camouflage techniques and survival. And Nero was, after all, a ghost; had been for years. A little hide-and-seek in the forest was nothing for him.

"How did you find us?" I asked.

He waved me off. "You've been driving with a tracker on your car for the last week or so. Harry, when I prepare, I prepare thoroughly."

I nodded. "The smoke screen was unexpected, I'll give you that. How did you manage to do it, Albert? We didn't give you that much time, did we?"

He let out a short laugh. "Oh, I had all the time in the world, Harry. I learned about Casey's involvement in the Senator's schedule weeks ago."

"And?"

Albert became animated then, as if he was a movie director and I'd just asked him the most interesting question. He said, "As soon as I heard Casey was involved, I got to work. Every location Senator Hawke was going to, I'd be with him. It's a long story, but you get the idea. Prep ahead. Prep well."

He winked at the Senator like a salesman who'd just delivered a pitch. Hawke nodded absently; he looked spaced out, maybe in shock. I was getting worried about him.

Albert's suit was its own peculiarity, too: it was similar to a military wetsuit issued to the U.S. Navy SEALs: a dull black suit with a horizontal front zip at the chest and a hood. Black was the operative word: it was so black it seemed to suck in what little light there was.

"It's manta black," he said, reading my thoughts. "Swanky, right? It's a recent upgrade... Anyway, did you find Wu's rifle yet? Or Simon's pills?"

"Not sure," I said, secretly glad I'd nailed the pills part. "She had a rifle? I didn't know that. Let me guess, she hid it in a tree?"

"Bingo, Harry. I can see why you pay yourself the big bucks."

I was coming to realize Albert had a very punchable face. I said, "So, Wilder was hooked on Adderall, and he got his supply from Hammerhead at Hangar Town?"

"Yeah, that was his fix. Said it kept him calm and focused, especially before a job. I told him it wouldn't end well..."

He was leaning on the car, visibly impatient, while Senator Hawke, now standing next to me, looked on, awkwardly, a third wheel in a conversation between two... Killers? Mercenaries? I didn't want to answer that question. I still thought of Albert Westwood as Nero, an assassin, a killer for hire.

"Senator," I said, "can I get you something? Some water, maybe?"

"No, Mr. Starke, I appreciate the thought. No, I'd like to find my wife... *now*."

"Ah, but of course!" Westwood said. "Might I suggest a more comfortable location, however?"

"Senator?" I said. Technically, he was still my employer.

"I agree with Mister..."

"Westwood. Albert Westwood. Pleased to meet you, sir."

"Andrew Hawke."

They shook hands. I tensed, but Westwood seemed calm, friendly, so I relaxed, a little.

"I could use a drink," I said, "and I know just the place, a place where we won't be disturbed."

"Shouldn't we alert the police first?" Senator Hawke asked. I took his unnatural calmness as his way of maintaining self-control. He stood motionless, as if in a dream.

"We should," Westwood said, "but not from either of your phones. I'd wager Wu is listening. Tell you what, mate, I'll meet you at this... place, yeah? And I'll call the police, don't you worry about that."

Hawke looked at me, and I gave him a nod, told Westwood where we were going, and then I put Senator Hawke in the rear seat behind me; by then, Albert Westwood had disappeared into the night.

"Do you trust that man, Harry?"

"Not in the slightest, Senator, but he is our best bet for finding your wife. He knows Casey Wu, knows how she thinks, operates."

"And you don't?" he asked, and his tone told me he was just talking, not trying to wind me up.

"No," I said, admitting defeat. "I thought I did, but look how that worked out."

Hawke didn't say anything. Like me, he was probably thinking, *What the hell have I gotten myself into?*

I couldn't blame him. Me? Well, despite the man's wife having been kidnapped, and now having to deal with a man I knew to be a contract killer, I was surprisingly upbeat.

We didn't talk much on our way to the Sorbonne—where else?—and I was the happier for it. I had a number of questions for our new frenemy, but I wanted to ask them in a more controlled environment, and Benny's bar was as good a place as any.

Would this be another trap? Would I once again be trusting a secretive, ex-military assassin with my life and the life of the Senator? Maybe, but this time I actually had a good feeling about it. If Nero wanted to kill us, he could've done so back at the trailer park, with no witnesses and no one to come to our rescue. What else could he need? Casey Wu? Sure, but did he really need my help for that? He could've killed us all back at the park, now that I think about it. What did he care about MaryAnne?

"We're here," I announced to Hawke as I parked at the curb.

"Hey, Harry!" Laura greeted us as we stepped inside the almost deserted bar.

"Oh, hey handsome," she said, looking over my shoulder.

I turned quickly, my hand inside my jacket.

"Easy, Harry," Westwood said, his hands raised in front of his chest, palms out. "Hey, yourself, lovely lady."

I swear Laura's cheeks flushed, and she bit her lower lip. I'd never seen her so genuinely taken with anyone. I felt a little jealous.

Albert, a thin cigarette between his lips, had changed out of his tactical suit into jeans, a black shirt, and a denim jacket. With his receding hair he not only sounded like Jason Statham, but he even looked a little like him.

"I need somewhere private, where we can talk," I told her.

"This is as private as you're gonna get, Harry. Grab a booth."

If she recognized the Senator, she didn't say so, nor did she mention the attempt on his life, though she must have known about it. It had to have been all over the news. I'd also been worried that the patrons would recognize Hawke, but I needn't have; what few there were, were too drunk to pay us any attention.

I steered Westwood and the Senator to a corner booth at the far wall. Hawke and I ordered scotch; Westwood ordered a bottle of light beer.

"I prefer clarity of mind," he said, leaning back, one hand inside his jacket—on the grip of a weapon, I assumed—the other on the table.

Looking back on it, I should've ordered a beer too, but who knew?

Laura, God bless her soul, brought me some real scotch, not the watered-down crap Benny Hinkle usually sold, and I took a large sip. *Oh geez, did I ever need that.*

The Senator's hand shook violently as he raised his glass to his lips, but soon settled as the fiery liquid did its job, though he still seemed to be in a trance, his thoughts far away from us. I felt infinitely sorry for him. Sure, he chose to live a public life, but neither he nor MaryAnne deserved what had just happened to them.

"I'll find her, Andrew. I promise." I looked sideways at Westwood. There was a tight smile on his lips.

"Isn't that right, Nero?"

He shrugged, the smile broadened, mocking, and he said, "Maybe."

I turned back to Hawke. "Not maybe. It's a promise."

Hawke nodded, absently staring at his hands wrapped around his glass on the tabletop. Then he looked up at me, held my gaze and said, without humor, "A promise? You seem to forget that I'm a politician, Mr. Starke. I know what promises are worth."

Westwood laughed. "You got that right, mate."

"I need you to come with me to the police department, Albert. I need you to make a statement. I want everything you have on Wu."

He studied his beer for a moment, took a sip, looked sideways at me, and said, "All right, I can do that."

That was unexpected. "Good, good. I'll let them know we're coming in, then."

"Yeah, go ahead," he said.

I took out my iPhone and stepped away from the booth to call Kate.

"Harry? Where the hell are you?" she asked.

"Out with some friends."

"Those friends wouldn't include Senator Hawke by any chance? Listen, I don't have time for this. What happened at the trailer park?"

I let out a breath, not sure where to start. "A lot of things. The safehouse was attacked, for one and... Look, it'd be better if I told you everything in person. Where are you?"

"I'm driving."

"Right. Well, I was about to take Westwood to Amnicola to make a statement, but it's probably better if we meet at my office."

She didn't answer.

"Kate?"

"Yes, Harry?" she said impatiently.

"Did you hear? He's with us. Nero!"

There was a long pause, and I started to think we got disconnected. "Kate?"

"Let me get this straight. Roger Booker's secret safehouse got attacked, and now you're hanging out with Senator Hawke and the guy someone hired to kill him?"

"Nero wasn't hired to kill him," I replied, watching Westwood, leaning on the table, conversing with the Senator.

"Like I said, it's a long story. Meet me at the office in half an hour, okay? We're on our way."

I clicked off and returned to the table, downed what was left of my scotch, took a fifty-dollar bill from my wallet, dropped it on the table and said, "Let's go."

"Already?" Westwood said. It wasn't really a question.

We left the bar without saying goodbye to Laura and stopped on the sidewalk to take in some fresh air. Westwood glanced at his watch.

"Thanks for the drink, lads," he said. "Bloody nice of you, Harry."

I narrowed my eyes. Something was not right.

"Harry, before I go, there's something I wanted to ask you. Have you looked into the man who hired Wu and her team? Cause I think you should."

Before I go...

I put a hand on the roof of the Maxima, suddenly feeling much drunker than I should've.

"What are you doing—"

"I'm not doing squat, mate," he said, interrupting me. "But you... Looks like you've had a little too much to drink, yeah?"

Senator Hawke looked worried. I had to grab onto his elbow to stay on my feet.

"Drink some water, old lad, when you come to... You didn't really think I'd go to the fuzz with you, did you,

Harry? Silly man. What were you thinking? But I'm not angry with you, the beer was tolerable, and I did have a nice time. We'll see each other again soon, yeah? And we'll find Casey, and your good lady, Senator."

He patted my shoulder and then walked away into the darkness... or maybe I simply passed out.

24

I came to with a hangover, and angry... No, not angry—totally pissed. At Nero? You betcha, but more with myself for trusting him, for being drugged like a naive college girl and then being left on the sidewalk like a sack of...

But I wasn't on the sidewalk, not when I awoke. I was lying in the back seat of a car... but it wasn't moving... *Wait, it's my car!*

I recognized the smell, and I recognized the magazine tucked in the back pocket of the driver's seat—an outdated issue about fancy boats, probably left there and forgotten by August months ago.

"Hawke?" I said.

The man in the passenger seat turned to look at me and said, "You're alive, thank God! You just keeled over. I didn't know what to do, so I put you in your car. I was about to call 911, but me being who I am... and..."

"It's okay. How long was I out for?"

"Not long. About thirty minutes, I think. It's after two-thirty in the morning."

"Jesus," I muttered, forcing myself to sit up.

My thoughts were a jumbled mess, and my insides felt even worse. Whatever Nero had given me—and, yeah, he lost the privilege of being called by his real name as quickly as he'd gotten it—whatever he'd given me didn't agree with the scotch, and I hadn't eaten all day.

I needed Kate, and I wasn't too proud to admit it. I took out my phone and dialed her number.

"You're at your office? I'll be right there, Harry," she said.

"No, not the office. I'm with Hawke, in my car outside the Sorbonne, and I'm not fit to drive."

I heard tires screech on the other end. "You've been drinking? What the hell, Harry?"

"No, not that, just... It's part of that long story I promised to tell you."

"That's not good enough, Harry. What are you and the Senator doing at the Sorbonne, and where's his wife? Does Booker know?"

"Kate, please," I replied, too tired and hungover to argue over the phone. "Just come and get us, okay?"

I clicked off and rolled onto my back. If you told me I'd been hit by a truck, I would have believed you.

"Did Nero say anything else when he left?" I asked.

"No," Hawke replied. "He's gone. What are we going to do about finding MaryAnne, Harry? I'm strongly considering getting the FBI involved."

I closed my eyes. Hawke was right. Hell, any sensible person would've called the cops back at the trailer park. But Hawke hadn't, nor did he display any real signs of worry or stress. He seemed perfectly calm. Was it part of his makeup? Maybe, but maybe it was something else... *What the hell's his game?*

"What's your game, Senator?" I heard myself say.

Hawke didn't reply for a long moment. Then, he said, "They say politicians only lie when they open their mouths, don't they?"

"Right."

"Harry, *I'm* telling you the truth when I tell you I'm terrified. I don't know what to do. For the first time in my career, in my life, I'm completely out of my depth. My wife's been kidnapped, there's been an attempt on my life, my bodyguards murdered... I don't know who I can trust. What I do know is that you're the only one *I can* trust, and we don't have much time. If anyone can find Mary-Anne and get us out of this mess, it's you. So what would you have me do?"

I took a deep breath and stared up at the roof of my car, trying to clear the fog from my brain.

What Hawke had said rang true; I believed him. The man sitting in the passenger seat was no longer a politician, just a man, a husband scared out of his mind. But Hawke was smart, too, and calculating—he knew the protocol. He knew that if he called the police, or the FBI, or even Booker, Casey Wu would know, and things would get very complicated very quickly. No, he figured that I was his only hope.

I nodded—pain speared through my head. I thought my eyeballs were going to explode. *What the hell did that son of a bitch give me?*

"We'll get it done," I said, with more confidence than I felt. "The best thing we can do now is to wait for Wu to contact us, find out what she wants, make sure MaryAnne is... safe." I almost said 'make sure she's still alive,' but thought better of it. "They always want something."

"She wants me, doesn't she?" he asked.

I turned my head to look at him. His face was dark, in shadow, but somehow he still looked strangely calm. I nodded.

He nodded too, and then he passed me a bottle of water, which I inhaled, and then the interior of the car was illuminated by bright white headlights.

I sat up again, sort of, opened the car door, and tried to get out, and then Kate was at my side, helping me to stand up. The fresh air hit me like a cool wave. We stood together for a moment, she had her arm around my waist; I had mine around her shoulder... *Wow, I never realized just how tall she is.*

We stood for a long minute while I gathered myself together, then I kissed her gently on the lips and released her.

"Thank you for coming, Kate." I turned to Hawke, who was now out of the car and standing next to the open passenger door.

"Of course," she said. "Now, talk to me. Tell me what happened."

I nodded, leaned back against the car, breathing the cool, early morning air, trying to block out the cacophony of crappy music emanating from within the Sorbonne. And then I proceeded to describe the events of the past several hours; Hawke corroborating my story sounding, even to me, as if he was trying to cover my ass. Which, of course, he was, and she listened intently without interrupting.

It was an embarrassing tale I told that left Kate cupping her face in her left hand and shaking a finger at me with her right.

For what seemed like an age, she was speechless,

gobsmacked. Then, with her eyes closed, she said, "I need a minute here, Harry."

I nodded and watched the expressions passing across her face as she processed what I'd just told her.

Then she opened her eyes and said, "So, what you're telling me is that, even though he drugged you and left you on the side of the road, you're convinced Nero is a good guy?"

"It wasn't quite that dramatic, but yes."

"Senator Hawke?" she said.

"Please, call me Andrew, both of you. I don't know about that Nero person. All I know is that woman has my wife. What are we going to do? We have to find her. Please?"

"And we will," I said. "I promise. Nero said we should look into Booker, since he's the one who hired TSA in the first place."

"Haven't you looked into that already?" Kate asked.

I was about to answer when my phone beeped. It was Jacque, and her message was short: *Bob is awake! So is Tim!*

"We need to go to the hospital," I said. "Bob and Tim are awake."

25

I had Hawke drive my car to the hospital, which he agreed to do without protest. Kate followed behind us. Less than ten minutes later, we arrived at Erlanger; it was just after three-thirty. Two cups of crappy vending machine coffee later and I could almost think straight, and I was able to walk without support, just.

"Harry!" Tim shouted as we stepped out of the elevator.

His head was bandaged, but my favorite hacker had a lively spring in his step and a smile on his face. *Geez, does nothing ever phase the kid?*

He grabbed Kate and gave her a hug.

"I'm so happy to see you up and about, Tim," she said. "How are you feeling?"

"A bit shook up, but I'll live. Did you get her?"

I shook my head. "No, but she didn't get us, either. Nero got Donald, though, with a sniper rifle."

"Oh, wow," Tim said. "You know, I don't think Donald was a bad guy."

Not thinking clearly, I said, "No? He mowed down two of Senator Hawke's bodyguards before Nero took him out, so there's that."

Tim stared at me, aghast; hell, everyone stared at me, including the Senator. It wasn't something I should have said, considering Tim's fragile condition, and I immediately felt like an idiot for being so crass. Fortunately, Jacque came to my rescue.

"Harry," she said, as she stepped out of a room a little farther along the corridor. "Kate, Senator. Thank goodness you're here. So, are y'all gonna come visit Bob or what?"

She stood back and ushered us into Bob's room—me last—where a nurse was fiddling with his IV.

As I was about to enter, Jacque put a hand on my arm and pulled me to one side.

"What has happened to you, man? You look like d'devil just kicked you out of hell."

I smiled at her, put an arm around her shoulder, pulled her to me, hugged her and kissed her on her forehead.

"It's a long story," I said. "Too long, but I'm fine... at least I will be when I've had some sleep. How's Bob doing?"

She sighed, tilted her head slightly to one side, and said, "Well, he's awake... Oh, Harry. I'm so worried about him. Please go talk to him."

So I did.

For some reason—hoping against hope, I suppose—I'd expected to find my friend wide awake and animated, ready to joke around and... Well, the reality was upsetting: his eyes were open and he was breathing, barely. Most of his face was covered with an oxygen mask. His torso was heavily bandaged, and an IV stood like a sentinel beside him, fluid drip, drip, dripping as the monitors beeped and blinked around him.

"Hey, man," I said, sitting in a chair next to him.

He blinked.

"What the hell d'you think you're doing lying around like this?" I asked. "It's not Sunday. You're supposed to be at work."

I saw the smile in his eyes and I knew he was going to be all right.

Kate put a hand on his.

"The doctor said the wound itself is not critical," Jacque said, in a whisper, "but he lost alotta blood, him lyin' out there all alone for so long, bleedin', so that's a good thing, right?"

"It is," I agreed bitterly, my eyes watering. "I'll make it up to you, buddy. I'll catch the bastard and put him away; bet on it."

Again, I caught the smile in his eyes, then he blinked and looked at Senator Hawke standing with his arms folded just inside the room, beside the door.

"I wanted to thank you, Mr. Ryan," Hawke said, quietly, "for risking your life for me. I'll make it up to you. You too, Mr. Clarke."

"Just doing my job, sir," Tim said with a grin.

"May I have a moment, please, Senator? Sir?" Kate said.

Hawke nodded, opened the door and followed her out into the corridor.

Jacque, Tim, and I spent a few more minutes with Bob before he drifted off to sleep. I was feeling a little better about him, but I had no doubt he was going to be out of commission for the foreseeable future. We crept quietly out of the room into the corridor where Kate and the Senator were waiting for us.

"We're going to the PD, Harry, Senator Hawke and I. You can tag along if you want, or you can catch some sleep and come in first thing in the morning. But *don't* screw me over."

I nodded and said, "I'll see you in a couple of hours."

She was serious, and I knew it. Had I been anyone else, she would've already hauled me in, so I was happy to cooperate. As always.

I checked my watch. It was almost four-thirty. "I'll go to my office, grab a couple of hours on the sofa and be there at nine."

We said our goodbyes, and I drove the couple of miles to my office, parked out front on the street, and let myself in through the front door.

By the time I got to my sofa, however, I was fully awake, my head clear, and I had something on my mind, and it wouldn't wait; I called Roger Booker.

He answered on the first ring. "Starke?" His tone was accusatory, and he waited for me to speak.

"I know, Roger. It's a mess. Look, I'm meeting Detective Gazzara at the PD on Amnicola at nine—"

"Good," he said, interrupting me. "I'll be there too."

"There is one thing I wanted to ask you, though," I said.

"What's that?"

"I need to speak with you in private before we meet at the PD. Can you do that?"

Booker paused, then sighed. "What d'you need to talk to me about? Another one of your crazy *sting operations*?"

"Not yet," I replied truthfully, "which is why I need your help."

"When? Where?"

"In my office, at eight?"

"I look forward to it," he said, the sarcasm plain to hear, and then he disconnected.

I fell onto the couch and was asleep before my head hit the pillow. The next thing I knew I was awakened by a loud knocking on the front door.

⁓

"It's five after eight, Mr. Starke," Booker said when I opened the front door to my outer office and let him in. He wasn't alone. The bodyguard at his shoulder was a giant, at least six-five and built like a brick chicken house.

"It's been a hell of a night," I replied. "May we speak in private?"

"What about my driver?" he asked, glancing sideways at the hulk.

"He can make coffee. It's through there. We won't be long."

I showed Booker into my private office.

He took a seat in front of my desk, looked me in the eye, and said, "Senator Hawke tells me you're not to blame for what's happened; I disagree."

I didn't speak. I wasn't about to defend myself, nor would I give him the satisfaction of agreeing with him. I had an idea Booker was himself in big trouble. He was, after all, ultimately responsible for the Hawkes' safety.

"Okay, let's get to it, Roger," I said. "Why did you hire TSA?"

He rolled his eyes. "Are you kidding me, Starke? You

can't seriously think I had any part in this mess? This is a courtesy visit, damn it. I shouldn't even be here—"

"And yet you are here, aren't you?" I asked, interrupting him. "So why are you here? To cover your ass?" I stood up from my chair and put my hands on the desk. "Let's not screw around anymore, shall we? I think you hired Casey Wu and her team to kill Senator Hawke."

Booker's eyes widened in shock; the color drained from his face. He opened and closed his mouth, twice, like a fish out of water. Finally, he whispered, "You're insane."

I sat back down and let him compose himself. When he did, I said, "No," while staring him right in the eye. "I don't think you did. What would your motive be?"

He looked at me, his eyes glinting. I continued, "But someone did have a motive... Didn't *she?*"

Booker swallowed, hard, and then said, "You can't be implying... MaryAnne would never..."

"MaryAnne would never what?" I pressed him.

"She would never want to see Andrew harmed... would she?"

I shrugged. "You tell me, Roger. Was it MaryAnne who hired TSA?"

Booker swallowed again and took a long moment to find his words. "She... she gave me Agent Wu's contact information, but I was the one who hired her."

I nodded, my suspicions confirmed. "So, she found TSA and ordered you to—"

"She didn't order me to do anything!" Booker snapped. "It was my decision to hire them after my team had thoroughly investigated Agent Wu and her people. Their records were clean. But..."

"But?"

"MaryAnne did recommend that I provide them with full access to..." He trailed off, shaking his head.

"I see. Thank you for sharing, Mr. Booker. Can I count on your support when I offer this theory at the meeting with the FBI this morning?"

Booker flexed his hands, sweating, nodding.

"Yes... but... but you have to understand..."

"I do."

I checked my watch. It was almost eight-thirty. We didn't have much time if we were going to make it to the meeting on time.

"We should go now, Roger. We wouldn't want to hold up MaryAnne's rescue operation, would we?" I asked sarcastically.

My sarcasm was lost on him. He jumped to his feet, looking at his watch, and said, "Yes, indeed."

At the front door, Booker's driver elbowed me out of the way, opened it, and looked this way and that, up and down the street, as if he was expecting an ambush. We walked out into the street, and I took out my iPhone to call Kate and let her know we were on the way.

"I'll see you there," I told Booker.

He nodded and headed to the SUV. The driver opened the door for him, and then stepped around the back of the car and slid into the driver's seat. The big V8 engine roared, there was a slight pause, and then, the SUV exploded in a spectacular ball of fire and black smoke.

26

Even though the SUV was parked several yards down the street, the blast wave of heat and debris drove me backward through the front door into my office. I stumbled, went down, dropping my phone, banging the back of my head against Jacque's desk. I rolled over, struggled to my feet, and staggered back outside again.

What was left of Booker's SUV was engulfed in flames. Parts of the vehicle, its hood, door, were scattered around all over the street, some pieces on fire, some smoking.

Shit! I ran to the SUV knowing full well that neither of its occupants could have survived the blast. I couldn't get within ten feet of it, but I could see the driver, burning furiously, slumped over the wheel. Booker... His already blackened outline was sitting upright in the passenger seat. *Oh, my God.*

I ran to my Maxima, swept smoking debris off the hood, and climbed inside to back it away. The front bumper had already begun to melt from the heat of the blaze. Only later did I realize how stupid that was—the Maxima could have been wired to explode, too. But I was in shock and running on a measly two hours of sleep.

I backed up the car about ten feet, stopped, and watched as the Cadillac continued to burn. People were beginning to gather, phones in hand, recording. I shuddered to think what would be on YouTube, probably even before the first responders arrived. I heard sirens; they were no more than a block away and coming fast.

The scene was about to get complicated with first responders and reporters. And there was nothing I could do for Booker. I waited a moment longer, and then slowly pulled away from the curb, made a U-turn, and drove away from the office, leaving the door wide open and—I realized a few moments later—my iPhone was still on the floor. As I said, my thinking was impaired.

I headed for Amnicola and the police department. Without my phone, I had no way of contacting Kate. I was now sure that MaryAnne Hawke was behind her husband's failed assassination and was working with Casey Wu. I also figured she must have approved Booker's murder, in which case she was getting desperate, angry, and more dangerous by the minute. I stepped on the gas.

Ten minutes later, after negotiating the worst rush hour traffic I'd known in more than a dozen years, I fishtailed the Maxima off Amnicola into the PD parking lot.

I parked the car, ran into the building, into the lobby, and then smack into the first line of bureaucracy: the receptionist, a young officer who insisted on filling out his form before agreeing to pick up the phone. Finally, he called Kate then handed the phone to me.

"What the hell just happened, Harry?" I swear she screamed it at me. I told her, but she'd already heard.

I handed the phone back to the clerk and he hit the button; there was a click, and I pushed the door open and rushed on through into the madhouse.

And madhouse was exactly what the conference room was. Filled to capacity, everyone talking at once, the room went suddenly quiet when I entered and everyone turned to stare at me. They were all there: Kate, Senator Hawke, Chief Johnston, Henry Finkle, even Sergeant Lonnie Guest, along with a dozen or so senior officers, detectives, and FBI agents.

"What the hell happened out there, Harry?" Chief Johnston asked.

I talked; they listened. I talked and I talked some more, for at least twenty minutes. One thing I didn't mention was my theory that MaryAnne Hawke was behind the plot to kill her husband. When I was done, they all sat there, staring at me, silently.

FBI Special Agent In Charge Georgina Powell, all business suit and hair bun, looked at me like I was some kind of rodent. Her look said it all: *Who the hell is this guy?* And I didn't blame her, not one bit. I was running on empty, barely two hours of sleep, and still wearing the same clothes I'd been wearing the day before. The last two days had been a rollercoaster, that was for damn sure... And, after what had just happened to Booker, I was exhausted.

Andrew Hawke was hit hard by the news of Roger Booker's death. They'd been friends for half a century, and I couldn't fathom the pain he must have been in. Still, he kept it together and kept listening.

"And just why did you want to meet Roger Booker

alone, Starke?" Finkle asked. He was angry, I could tell, but he was holding onto his emotions, trying not to embarrass himself in front of the federal agents.

"I wanted answers," I replied. "Truthful answers, without all this..." I paused and looked around the room, waved a hand at them all, then continued, dryly, "hullabaloo."

"And did you get those answers?" Powell asked, her arms folded, head down, staring at me through half-closed eyes.

I looked at Hawke, then at Kate, then back at Powell.

"Booker told me that MaryAnne Hawke was the person behind hiring Casey Wu and TSA."

Several people gasped. Finkle shouted, "What?" Powell stared at me open-mouthed. Hawke half rose to his feet, his hands on the table.

"Are you... are you saying that my wife tried to kill me?" His eyes were hard, chips of flint, and intensely focused on me. His brow was furrowed. He was angry, oh so angry. *But is he angry at me?* I wondered.

"I'm saying it's a possibility, Senator. That's what your chief of security told me. She gave him Wu's name and contact information and recommended he hire them." That last was a bit of a stretch, but what the hell?

"More Starke nonsense," Finkle snarled. "It's about time someone—"

Kate shot him a look.

"Shut up, Henry," Johnston snapped, cutting him off.

There was a moment of silence while everyone thought about what I'd said. Well, I assumed that's what they were doing.

Finally, Powell spoke, "We have only Starke's word that Mrs. Hawke is responsible for hiring TSA. Booker's dead, so we can't confirm it, but we can't dismiss it either. I know how you must be feeling, Senator Hawke, but we are obligated to look into it."

Hawke didn't move.

Powell clapped her hands. "All right, people! Let's get to work. Senator, I'm going to need your help."

He nodded, but then he said, "Will you give me a moment, Agent Powell? I need to get something to eat. I'll pass out if I don't." Then he looked at me.

I stared hard at him, wondering... *Are you trying to tell me something?*

Powell nodded respectfully and busied herself with her paperwork. Hawke excused himself.

I followed him out of the room and down the hallway to a small breakroom where a couple of vending machines stood together against the far wall. Hawke studied the selection of chips, chocolate bars, and cookies without much enthusiasm, then took out his wallet, peeked inside it, and cursed under his breath.

"What are you having?" I asked, ten bucks in my hand.

"Turkey Swiss, please," he said, pointing at a wrapped sandwich.

I fed the bill into the machine, punched in the code, and the sandwich fell into the hopper.

"Coffee?" I asked as I pressed the button to pour one for myself.

"Water will do," he replied, filling a paper cup from a cooler.

I waited for my coffee, and then we stepped over to one of three metal tables and sat down.

I said, "I'm sorry to be the bearer of bad news, Andrew. I—"

"Don't. Roger called me this morning, before he met with you, Mr. Starke. He may not have told you, but he thought very highly of you, and I trusted his judgment. I still do."

He spoke highly of me? Who would have thought it? Still...

There was nothing much to say that hadn't already been said before, so I remained silent.

"How sure are you that it's MaryAnne?" he asked quietly, nursing his cup of water, staring at it.

I didn't answer immediately. I thought about it, not quite as sure as I had been back at my office.

There were some obvious giveaways. For starters, Wu and Rockford had attacked the safehouse. How did they know Hawke and his wife were at the trailer park? Nero admitted he'd put a GPS tracker on my car. It made sense, then, that maybe Rockford had put one on the Senator's car, and Booker's too for that matter.

And why didn't they just go ahead and kill everyone inside the trailer? Rockford eliminated the two guards and then Casey Wu went in with a handgun and took MaryAnne hostage. She could have killed the Senator right there and then, but she didn't... Then again, on thinking about it, how could she? I had my gun on her; the minute she shot Hawke I would have killed her, so she took MaryAnne instead, decided to live to fight another day, maybe.

MaryAnne recommended Wu to Booker... that was a given. It had to be her. If not, her recommending Wu to Booker was a coincidence, and I don't believe in those, especially one as far out as this one would have been. No... but why? What was her motive?

"It's the only thing that makes sense," I said. "The

only thing I don't understand is why she'd want you dead?"

Hawke had unwrapped his sandwich and was devouring it like an animal, pieces of lettuce dropping out, his lips smeared with mayo. *Ugh!*

Luckily, no one was taking photos. If they had, it would have cost him at least a one-point drop in the polls.

Hawke washed down the last few bites of his breakfast and threw the wrapper and the paper cup into the trash can next to the machines. There was an air of resignation about his actions, as if whatever happened next was out of his hands—which it really was—and we had all the time in the world—which we really didn't.

Then he looked at me and said, wryly, "Why would she want me dead? She wouldn't... doesn't. She's innocent. She loves me. She didn't do it."

I couldn't believe what I was hearing. *Is the man insane?*

"You really believe that?" I said, not knowing what else to say.

"Oh, but I do. All that matters now is that MaryAnne comes home safely."

He paused, shrugged, then said, "I know why you followed me out here, Harry, and it wasn't for the horrendous coffee, was it?"

I didn't answer. I listened.

"I've watched you at work," Hawke said, "and I like to think my people's instincts are sharp. You make your own rules, and while I don't agree with that approach and cannot support it, I won't do anything to stop you, either. You want to go after Agent Wu, don't you? Alone, without, what did you call it? All this... hullabaloo."

I sipped my admittedly horrendous coffee and waited

for him to continue; there was something I wasn't quite getting.

"It's about the politics, Harry. That's what my life is all about. So, I'd like you to find my wife, as soon as possible, and return her to me... without involving Agent Powell or the police."

"You can't be serious?" I said, stunned. "After all she's done? After she's tried to have you killed? Seven people are dead, Senator. We can't let her get away with it... We can't."

"I told you, Harry. She didn't do it. Wu did."

"But she hired Wu."

"No she didn't, Booker did, and he's dead, much to my sorrow. Now we have to rescue my wife. So I'll ask you again, can you do it. Can you find her?"

I didn't answer, not for what seemed like an age as I tried to think it through. *Is the man playing with a full deck? Does he really believe his own bullshit?* I didn't know.

"I don't know, Senator. I don't even know if I should try. You have to understand: I'm convinced she wants you dead, that she convinced Booker to hire Wu. I'm also convinced that she won't give up until you are... dead."

"You're wrong, Harry. Trust me, I know my wife. She's innocent and in great danger... Please find her for me."

Trust him? That's political speak for "not a word I'm saying is true."

"Can I ask you a question, Senator?"

"Ask away."

"Let me preface it by saying that I don't believe you. That there's a reason you want me to find her, just me, which is crazy when you can call on every law enforcement agency in the country to do it. So the question is... why?"

A bitter smile touched his lips. "Politics, of course," he said. "I still have an election to win, Harry. So far, I've won a lot of points... The electorate loves me. Can you imagine what will happen if even a hint of a rumor was to get out that my wife hired a private security firm to kill me? I won't have it, Harry. It needs to be done quickly and quietly."

Politics? I should have known. When he put it like that, I understood his logic... well, sort of.

"We need heroics," he said thoughtfully. His voice hardened, "We need to spin—"

"Spin?" I asked. *What the hell are you talking about?*

"I loved Roger like a brother, Harry," he said, "but we have to carry on, do we not? Now, please, find and return my wife to me safely, before the FBI has a chance to intervene."

"And if I don't?" I said, holding his gaze.

He smiled and said, "You owe me, Harry. If you hadn't screwed up, we wouldn't be in this predicament and my wife would be at my side, as always. Roger would still be alive and your own people... well."

I finished my coffee and threw the cup away, forcing myself to think. In truth, I could have used some sleep, preferably in my own bed. But, as they say, the job ain't over until the fat lady sings... In this case, the fat lady was the Senator's wife—not that she was fat, but she would keep trying to kill her husband—whether I liked it or not. I was convinced of it. *But what to do?*

I nodded, reluctantly, and said, "Fine, I'll find her. I'll bring her home, Andrew."

"Thank you, Harry," Hawke replied with a small

smile—he was already slipping back into the role of the agitated husband.

"You know her better than anyone," I said, trying to suppress a yawn. "Do you have any idea where she might be?"

"I can't speak for Agent Wu, as I've not had much contact with her, but I can tell you about my wife..."

And he did. Mostly the usual fluff you would read on Wikipedia or hear on a late-night talk show: how young Andrew met young MaryAnne, how they fell madly in love. On and on it went, until he mentioned Chattanooga.

"I love it here, Harry, this entire area, and so does MaryAnne. Mesmerizing scenery, nature, friendly people, for the most part. We even had our own special place here."

"A romantic getaway?" I asked, suddenly interested.

"You could say that, I suppose. We were married here, you know, in an old church on Williams Street. It's derelict now. There was some talk about turning it into luxury apartments, but it didn't happen, not yet anyway. We were just kids, no money, straight out of college..."

He was reminiscing, lost in the past. I had to bring him back to reality.

"Where?"

"Huh?"

"Where is your special place?"

"Oh, that. There's a motel we used to go to when... well, you know, off Old Lee Highway in Ooltewah, just north of Apison Pike. Before it closed down, we sometimes used to go back there. Stay in the motel, go to the drive-in to recapture old times." He shrugged.

I knew where he was talking about. It was one of those full-service Holiday Park Inns that went the way of the dodo bird. For more years than I can count, it struggled to stay open but finally closed for good in 2007, along with the Athenian Drive-In next door. It had been a busy place before I-75 was built. All gone today, of course, replaced by a fifty-acre subdivision, but in 2012 it was still there, derelict, and no longer in business.

"I know the place," I said.

"But Wu doesn't know about it. She wouldn't have taken MaryAnne there."

"Let's suppose, just for a moment," I said, thinking hard. "Now hear me out, Senator. Let's suppose MaryAnne's calling the shots, that Wu's working for her. You know your wife better than me. Is it somewhere she'd be likely to go?"

He made a weird face, shrugged. "I don't know. Maybe. I just want my wife back," he said plaintively.

Of course you do, I thought, dryly. *Time for me to get out of here, I think.*

"I'll be seeing you around, *Senator*, after I find your wife," I said, rising to my feet. I looked down at him, then walked quickly out of the breakroom. I wanted to get away before Agent Powell or Kate thought to send someone to bring us back to the conference room. I made a mental note to send Kate a message, and then I made another note, to get a new phone, as the old one would no doubt have been found in the lobby of my office.

I walked quickly down the hallway, past the conference room, and out of the building, not so fast as to attract attention, but quickly enough to get out of there unnoticed.

I stepped outside, started toward the parking area... and froze. The Maxima wasn't where I'd left it. *What... the hell?*

I was about to return to the reception desk and ask if it had been towed, for some obscure reason, when I saw it, coming north on Amnicola. It turned slowly into the lot and rolled to a stop in front of me. The passenger-side window rolled down, and Nero looked out at me from the driver's seat, grinning.

"Harry Starke?"

I glanced around, hoping no one was watching, then climbed in and slammed the passenger side door.

I rolled up the window as Nero circled back out onto Amnicola. *Does the son of a bitch ever sleep?* I wondered, idly.

He seemed lively enough, and well-rested. His eyes scanned the area constantly as he accelerated northward toward Highway 153. Oddly enough, I felt quite comfortable with him behind the wheel. And yet...

He glanced sideways at me and said, "Harry, I—"

I drove my fist into his face, hard. The car swerved violently. Nero steadied it, shook his head, and then rubbed his cheek.

"Oi, you. Punchin' the driver isn't kosher, mate! You do like to live dangerously, Harry Starke. I'll give you that."

"What the hell are you doing in my car?" I asked, shaking my hand: the bastard's skull must've been made of concrete.

"I figured you'd still be dizzy after the cocktail I gave you, so I thought I'd do the gentlemanly thing and drive you around."

"Not interested. Stop the damn car."

"Oh, come on, mate. You're not planning to go against Casey all by yourself, are you? You look like shit, and with that puny little M&P9? You don't stand a chance, mate. She's a frickin' pro."

I didn't say anything.

"How about this, Harry? You tell me where to go, and I'll back you, make sure you have the firepower you need."

Ah... what the hell? I thought. *Why not? I'm so deep in the shit right now, how much worse can it get?*

I kicked back in my seat, yawning. "Ooltewah, Old Lee Highway. Take I-75 to Exit 11. I'll guide you the rest of the way from there."

27

"I am glad you're feeling well, Harry, truly," Nero said as we sped along the on-ramp onto Highway 153. "I was worried you might have bought it."

"Oh, really?"

He shrugged. "You never know, do you? I mean, people react differently to drugs, yeah?"

"What the hell kind of assassin are you?" I said. "I thought they taught you better than that in the SAS."

"They did, but I'm a sniper, see? My specialty is long-range weapons, not poisons and shit. That stuff's too imprecise for my liking."

"I'm sorry I asked," I said dryly.

The sky was brightening, even so, I was having trouble staying awake. I rolled down the window; the cold, fresh air hit me like a hammer but didn't help much: a combination of whatever drug the clown sitting next to me had administered and lack of sleep, I supposed.

Nero was a good driver: disciplined, precise, and careful not to get spotted, yet driving slightly above the speed limit, through yellow lights, masterfully avoiding or slipping through the early morning traffic.

"You aren't much of a team player, are you?" I asked.

"Oh, I used to be. Not so much these days."

"I've noticed. Well, you better dust off those skills, Nero."

"The name's Albert, Harry," he said amiably. "Don't know about the team thing, though. You and I have different objectives. Mine is to kill Casey Wu."

Somehow, it didn't bother me. You know me, I'll take the perp in if I can, but I never lose much sleep if I don't, especially not if it's a sociopath like Wu.

"Did you know that it was MaryAnne Hawke who hired her?" I asked.

He shrugged. "I'm not surprised. The idea had crossed my mind, but that's immaterial. TSA is, was a bad lot, needs to be eliminated. Casey is the last of them."

"So, what is it?" I asked. "Some righteous crusade against your former colleagues?" I was starting to get a feel for Nero's thought process.

"Pretty much," he replied. "As long as Casey's alive, she'll be the angel of death and destruction. Changing the subject, I trust you're familiar with the layout of this... place, whatever it is?"

I would have liked to think so. The last time I'd been to the Athenian was more than thirty years ago, and I'd never stayed at the Holiday Park Inn.

"Yeah," I said, sarcastically, "know it like the back of my hand."

Nero glanced at me, unconvinced, and said, "I see. It's a good thing I've got the boot loaded with guns, then, eh?"

"You what?" I asked.

"We're going to war, Harry, old son. And I never go to war unprepared."

I sighed, both in frustration and because he was right. Casey Wu would be expecting us or, more likely, Nero. And she *would* be prepared. The only questions I had were: how deep was MaryAnne's involvement? Was she simply the mastermind, or an active participant? Would I be forced to kill Senator Hawke's wife? There was no scenario in which that would go well for me. I said as much to Nero, but he disregarded it, as I knew he would.

"Not my problem," he said.

And it wasn't; it was mine. No matter what happened, whatever the outcome, Nero could and would disappear when it was done, probably disabling me, leaving me to deal with the aftermath. Unless I got him first.

Look, I didn't dislike the guy; you couldn't, but he could be as annoying as hell and frankly, I'd had just about enough of his shit. I think he knew it, too. With my possible demise in the offing, then, I shut my mouth and began to formulate the obligatory plan. Don't I always?

~

"Okay," I said, "turn here and slow down. We're about two miles out." Two minutes later we'd arrived.

"Here," I said, "turn in here."

Oh yeah, now I remember, I thought as we turned onto a narrow road only to be forced to stop some twenty yards further on at a rusty steel gate that bore the missive: *No Access. Private Property. Keep Out.* Nero stopped the car close to the gate, almost too close, and stepped out to open it. I watched him. He was light on his feet, his movements precise and powerful, as he effortlessly lifted the gate and pushed it open. The next moment, he was back behind the wheel again.

"Someone's here," he said. "The chain's been cut."

"That means nothing," I said. "Could have been cut anytime, years ago."

"Not so, my friend," he said. "The cut steel was bright and shiny in the light of the headlights." And he turned them off. Fortunately, it was already light enough to see the road, what was left of it.

The road we were on had pretty much surrendered to the elements—the blacktop was cracked, uneven and in places overgrown. Nero slowed the car to a crawl as the road turned slightly to the right to reveal the Athenian's derelict box office, a vacant building, little more than a shed, its window glass long gone.

"Look familiar?" he asked.

"From what little I remember, yes. The motel should be round the next bend."

He nodded and drove on, past a clearing that used to be the parking area for the theater. It was piled high with scrap metal and trash, almost as high as the gutted movie screen beyond: a grid of steel and blackened wood, a grotesque skeleton silhouetted against the early morning sky.

The road made another, sharper, turn to the right, and there some five hundred yards on was the motel, what was left of it.

"Stop here," I said. "We should probably approach on foot."

Nero pulled over to the left, behind some low trees and bushes, turned off the motor, looked sideways at me, and said, "This is it, then, mate. You ready?" as he reached down and popped the trunk.

"Ready as I'll ever be."

I opened the car door and stepped out into the crisp morning air. Two deep breaths and I was feeling better. Not a new man, exactly, but decidedly better, refreshed and ready for... What? I had no idea.

"Come," Nero said as he stepped around to the trunk and lifted the lid.

I joined him and looked inside.

"Holy..." I said. "Are you frickin' crazy? What if we'd been stopped?"

Inside were four handguns, two sawed-off shotguns, and four semi-automatic rifles, spare magazines for all, three steel boxes full of ammunition, and two Kevlar vests.

"Take your pick, Harry," Nero said, and he went to get his sniper rifle hardcase from the back seat.

"Geez," I muttered, shaking my head, trying to imagine what might have happened if we'd been pulled over, the look on the officer's face when he discovered the arsenal in the trunk. Fortunately, it hadn't happened, yet.

I slipped out of my jacket and holster and put on one of the vests. It must have been one of Nero's because it was a little snugger than I would have preferred, but it would do the job.

My trusty Smith & Wesson was still in its holster. I slipped it out, checked the load—twelve, plus the one in the chamber, thirteen. Unfortunately, I had no spare mags with me. So, reluctantly, I set it down on the floor of the trunk and picked up a Glock 23, dropped the mag, checked the load, reinserted it, racked the slide, and pushed it into my shoulder holster. It was a bit tight, but it would do.

I put the holster on over the vest—the jacket I had to leave on the floor of the trunk. I stuffed two full Glock mags into my pants pocket, then I picked up a sawed-off shotgun, hefted it, and put it back. I don't like those things; they make too much mess. I settled instead for an AR15 semi-automatic rifle and one spare mag; that was it. If it wasn't enough... well, that didn't bear thinking about.

Meanwhile, while I was loading myself up, Nero was kneeling on the ground next to the car putting his rifle together.

"I'm going in through the lobby," I said. "Give me some cover."

He looked up, stared at me, then said, "I was planning something a little different, Harry."

"Sure you were, but you can forget it. We're going with my plan. You know, you've been such a pain in the ass, Nero, I ought to shoot you right here and now. Don't make me."

I didn't mean to threaten him with the AR, but it swung freely on my shoulder, its muzzle pointing at his face. He glanced at it, then back at me, smiling, nodded, and then went back to work on his rifle, saying, "Ah, bollocks."

"Give me a signal when you're in position."

Without another word, I pulled the Glock from its holster, turned and left him, wondering if he would follow my lead or stab me in the back? And by "stab" I meant a high-velocity rifle round through my chest; no, the Kevlar wouldn't stop that.

I walked quickly through the trees and shrubs, then ran, staying low, hurried across the one-time parking lot to the motel front entrance wall. And there I waited, listening: nothing.

I made my way slowly along the wall, staying low beneath the shattered windows, to the front door. There, I waited again, straining to hear even the slightest sound: again, I heard nothing.

Cautiously, I stepped into the lobby, cringing as the broken glass crackled and crunched beneath my feet. I froze, waiting for the impact of a bullet that never came.

It was rapidly getting lighter. The early morning sunlight illuminating the disaster that had once been the reception desk.

Our timing was all wrong for a rescue operation. Going in during daylight hours was a mistake. But it was too late to correct it. I was already committed. The big question now was, where the hell were they hiding?

I eased on through the lobby and into a corridor that provided access to the offices behind the front desk and found myself in a world of chaos, destruction, and decay. The office doors were gone. The offices themselves were empty of furniture; broken glass lay all over the floor.

Not here, that's for damn sure, I thought, and then cringed some more as the broken glass crunched underfoot. *They can't be here. Why would they? It's a nightmare. Maybe she couldn't think of anywhere else... Yeah, that makes sense... some.*

I continued on into the kitchen. The equipment, except for a couple of old refrigerators and an ancient gas range, was all long gone, replaced by piles of rotting cardboard boxes and mattresses that had once graced the guest rooms. Rusty steel bolts that had once held the kitchen tables in place stuck up out of the concrete. The room was an accident waiting to happen. The one-time dining room beyond was no different, an empty space littered with glass and debris.

My plan was painfully simple: go in, find Casey Wu and MaryAnne, and then play it by ear. If I could take them alive, great. If not... well, we'd have to see. But one way or another, I had to try to get MaryAnne out alive.

I stepped over to the bank of glassless windows, looking for Nero's signal. I saw nothing. *Damn! Where the hell is he?*

For all I knew, he'd decided to go it alone, come in with guns blazing, killing both Wu and Hawke's wife. And then I felt the skin on the back of my neck crawl as I realized, even as my mind was running amuck thinking of all the possible scenarios, his scope might be trained on my head. Involuntarily, I ducked down out of sight.

I shook it off; no point in worrying about something I couldn't change. I had to concentrate on the job at hand.

Nero's best bet, I figured, would be to find a vantage point ten or fifteen feet above ground and to the north, where he'd be able to watch both the inside of the building through the broken windows and the roof. That being so, I ventured out through the kitchen door.

I surveyed the terrain beyond the parking lot: nothing. *Crap! Where the hell are you?*

I looked to my right and spotted the same car I'd seen the night before. It was parked east of the dining room, off the lot, half-hidden among the undergrowth. *So you are here!*

I saw movement out of the corner of my eye—not inside the building, but away to the north, on top of a derelict garbage truck. *Nero!*

He was little more than a dark lump on top of the truck's compactor. I could make out the barrel of his rifle.

He must have seen me because he waved. *Thank you*, I waved back, ducked back inside the kitchen, tripped over one of the rusty floor bolts, staggered a little, and dropped to one knee, not a split second too soon.

Wu fired a burst from an automatic rifle from the door that led to the lounge, south of the dining room. The bullets tore at the wall above and behind me, shattering what little glass was left in the window, showering me with shards of filthy glass. My reflexes kicked in, and from the prone position I fired three times at the doorway, but Wu was no longer there. I jumped up and threw myself behind a pile of stinking mattresses.

"You need to leave, Starke!" she shouted.

"I'm here for Mrs. Hawke!" I shouted back, ducking for cover as she opened fire again.

"Come get her, then!" Wu said. "And bring that stupid mutt Nero with you!"

Barely had she gotten the words out than a bullet slammed into the concrete wall on the far side of the bar.

"Better luck next time—"

Another shot cut her off. I heard a sharp crack as the bullet struck metal, followed a split second later as the bullet careened off and struck something else, somewhere in the back of the lounge. I heard something drop to the floor, something metal, and I heard her curse: "Oh shit... Shit!"

Could it be? Had Nero really hit her weapon?

"Stay away!" she yelled, and then I heard steps, running.

"I'm going in!" I shouted, knowing Nero wouldn't hear me but hoping she would and, more importantly, believe it.

I wasn't sure if Nero could see me, but instead of

rushing after her, I exited the kitchen, out into the parking lot, and ran east, circled around the rear of the building, and then ran west along the south side of the building. With Nero covering the north side, Casey was now trapped, which was no advantage for me. You know what they say about trapped rats. She'd be waiting for me, of that I was sure.

Once again my strategy was a gamble: go in from the far side and surprise her, hence my run around the building. So far, so good.

There were no windows in the south wall, so there was no longer any need to duck. There was a door some fifty feet to the west, a staff entrance left slightly ajar. A trap? Only one way to find out. I took a deep breath and instead of creeping in slowly, warily, which I figured was what she'd expect me to do, I ran through the door at full speed, flung myself to the ground inside a darkened corridor, rolled, and brought my Glock to shooting position.

28

And... I felt like an idiot. There was no one there. I was lying on my back, Glock pushed forward in both hands, swinging it first to one side then the other, in a short, narrow hallway with two doors on each side and a fifth in front of me.

I stood and began opening doors, much more cautiously this time. I had no doubt that Wu had heard my dramatic entrance and was waiting for me... somewhere.

One of the doors on my left led to the lounge, the other, lined with empty shelves, was obviously a janitor's closet. The two doors on my right were the restrooms. Although neither had a sign, they were both open, and I could see the dirty toilet bowls and urinals against the far wall.

The hallway smelled dank and nasty.

I stood motionless for a moment, listening. I swept the empty restrooms with my gun. They'd be a perfect hiding place, but if Wu had been inside, she would have attacked immediately, making good use of the element of surprise.

I doubt I'd have had time to react. But, like the broom closet, they were empty, filthy... derelict, had been for years. I ignored the door to the lounge, focusing instead on the fifth door. I figured it would take me back into the kitchen—either that or what had once been the dining room and, presumably, Wu.

I stepped deeper into the hallway, leading with my gun. I put my ear to the door, heard whispers on the other side... or did I? Was it Wu talking to herself or with Mary-Anne, or was it just my imagination? Maybe it was either one or both of them waiting for me on the other side, ready to shoot? There was no way to know. There was only one way to find out. I took a step back, found my balance, and kicked in the door.

Two things happened. First, the door swung inward and banged against the wall like a gunshot. Second, the Glock was kicked out of my hands.

As if in slow motion, it flew up in the air, spinning end over end, almost to the kitchen ceiling. My reaction was to follow its flight: bad mistake. I didn't see it fall, because Casey Wu kicked me in the gut, knocking the wind out of me. As I folded, she swept my feet out from under me. I went down hard onto the dusty floor, the AR15 under my shoulder blade sending spears of pain shooting down my spine.

I discarded the AR and managed to block Wu's next kick with my hands, sweeping her leg away. I kicked at her ankles, bringing her down to my level. I rolled sideways and jumped to my feet, as did she, her hands up, ready to strike.

"You're dead, Starke," she hissed at me.

I had to crack a smile. Her right hand was missing the middle finger—the impact of Nero's bullet on the M4?—

and yet her confidence was boundless. I couldn't help but admire her tenacity.

"Not yet," I replied, taking a half-step forward and swinging at her with my left.

Oh, but she was fast. She ducked under my arm, landed a solid punch to my kidney that almost put me down again, dropped to her knees, grabbed the AR, rolled, and brought it to bear on my face. Fortunately for me, her injured right hand wasn't working too well—maybe she couldn't feel anything—and she had to look down to find the trigger.

My reflexes were on point that day. I ducked sideways, lunged at her, reached for the gun with my right hand and managed to grab onto the magazine, releasing it just as she pulled the trigger: BAM! I actually felt the muzzle flash burn my cheek, then: *Click,* nothing.

I punched the gun out of her hand, skinning my knuckles, but I didn't feel a thing; the adrenaline was pumping hard. She punched me in the ear, knocking me sideways, and then, twisting like she was made of rubber, she was out of my reach, turning, snarling like a wounded dog, and just as dangerous.

I threw the thirty-round magazine at her head, but she dodged it, her lips drawn back in a snarl showing her teeth, furious. Then she took a step back. The snarl turned into a smile that sent chills down my spine. She circled to the right, her hands high in front of her face, a rattler readying itself to strike. I stood upright, my hands balled into fists, agonizingly aware of the hazards built into the kitchen floor, but I didn't dare look down, not even for a second.

"I'm better than you, Harry," she said, and, without

waiting for an answer, she lunged at me. No, she flew at me like some sort of feral cat, snarling, spitting.

She went for my face with her nails, but missed, scratching my neck instead. I seized her left hand and, using her own momentum against her, pulled her through, launching her high into the air, spinning, to land on her back, winded.

"What the hell did they teach you at Quantico, *Agent*?" I asked sarcastically. That title now sounded weird to me.

I steadied myself, stood back, looked down at her, listening for other threats. MaryAnne Hawke was still out there somewhere. But I heard nothing, other than Casey Wu panting on the floor.

"Ready to go now?" I asked, taking a step sideways, controlling the space. There was nowhere for her to run: she was boxed into a corner, but there was still plenty of fight left in her.

She sat, then stood, slowly, with difficulty, fists clenched in front of her face.

"Stay away!" she shouted. And then she was in the air, flying toward me, feet first. I swear she leaped her own height.

But I was ready for her. I simply took a step to my left and she flew past, landing on her back again.

"Not good enough, sister," I said, smiling down at her.

She coughed, then gasped. "Go screw yourself, Starke."

And then she got lucky. She swung her right heel in a wide arc. It slammed like a hammer into my left knee, and I stumbled backward and fell, rolling, pain shooting through my ankle as it found one of those damned floor bolts... I also found something else. My Glock.

Wu jumped to her feet, slipped her right hand into her pants pocket and brought out a small pistol, a .22. Not much of a weapon, but in the right hands it would do the job, and Wu's were the right hands.

She took a step back, swapped the gun from her right to her left hand and pointed it at me, her right hand bleeding profusely. The only reason she didn't pull the trigger was because I was pointing my Glock 23 right back at her.

"You're outmatched, Casey. Give it up."

"Like hell, I will," she hissed, still catching her breath, and then she stepped quickly backward, out of the kitchen into the lounge.

"Stop, Casey," I shouted. "Don't make me kill you."

But she was gone.

29

I wondered if there was another part of the building where MaryAnne was hiding; the old guest rooms, maybe. But then, I heard the familiar, sharp, suppressed cracks of Nero's sniper rifle and glass shattering somewhere deeper within the building, beyond the lounge. Immediately after, I heard Casey Wu curse and shout, "Nero, you bastard!"

I jumped through the kitchen door into the corridor, took cover behind a corner, my back to the wall, and peeked into the lounge.

"Casey!" I shouted.

Nero had ceased fire. I peeked around the corner, Glock in hand. There was a door behind what once had been the lounge bar. It led into a back room that must once have been a staff locker room. A rusty locker door was swinging loose, its hinges creaking. The sun was up, streaming in through the glassless windows, motes of dust dancing in the sunbeams. Casey was back against the far wall, out of Nero's view through the shattered windows.

"Quit it, Nero!" she yelled. From the strain in her voice, I could tell she was hurt.

Nero fired again. The bullet slammed into the wall just a few feet to my left. *Dammit.*

"Casey," I shouted. "It's over. Give it up. I'll tell him to stop."

She laughed out loud, as if I'd just told her the funniest joke she'd ever heard. "I seriously doubt he'll do that, Starke."

"Either that, or he'll kill you."

"Or I'll kill him."

"Is that a gamble you're willing to take? He's been on you every step of the way, you and your little band of assholes. Three down, one to go, by my count."

"I could say the same about you, Harry," she yelled.

"Except, my guys are still alive and I'm not the one pinned down in this godforsaken nightmare of a motel... What've you done with MaryAnne? Is she safe?"

"Ooh, who's to say, Harry? For all you know, I could have strung her up in one of the restrooms. Why don't you go take a look?"

She was baiting me, as I was her. She was cornered, her back against the wall, legs apart, hands together between her legs, holding the .22 handgun. Yes, she was cornered, but so was I. The minute I stepped out of my cover, she'd have me. And then there was Nero out there somewhere. I didn't trust him not to take us both out. I stepped back into the corridor and pondered my predicament. I was at a loss. For several minutes I stood there, thinking; there was not a sound to be heard.

What the hell's Nero up to?

It was a stand-off, unless... Ah, what the hell... I took a deep breath and stepped quickly around the corner and into the room, my Glock pointed at Wu, who was now seated on the floor, her back against the wall, legs stretched out in front of her, the gun on the floor between her legs. She looked up at me, her injured right hand on her stomach, her left hand covering the right.

I stepped toward her, raised my left hand, palm-out at the window, hoping Nero would see it. He must have because he didn't shoot.

"Let's go, Casey," I said. "You're safe."

She smiled, weakly, brushed back her hair with her left hand and said, "You really are stupid, Harry. You're in bed with Nero now, but the moment you turn your back on him, he'll stab you."

"He hasn't yet," I replied.

"Yet."

There was a narrow hallway to her left, presumably leading to the staff entrance. She glanced round at it, then back at me; she still wasn't ready to quit.

"Get on the floor, Casey, face down."

She looked up at me, pleading, desperate. She began to pivot to lay down. For a second the gun on the floor between her legs was out of my sight, but then she rolled to her right, the small gun in her left hand and at the same instant, she scissor-kicked her legs, twisting in the air like a damned gymnast, and kicked the Glock upward just as I pulled the trigger. The bullet slammed into the concrete wall just inches above her head.

I didn't see her shoot, but I heard it: a crack no louder than a champagne cork. At first I felt nothing; it took a second for my leg to register the pain, and then I went down. She'd hit me in my lower calf, right leg.

Nero must have seen what happened because he started shooting again. A bullet smashed into the concrete floor, ricocheting across the room, hitting the wooden door frame, tearing a huge chunk of wood loose. I waited, he fired again, higher this time; the round hit the wall opposite the window and went clean through. He fired again. I was down, flat on the floor, on my stomach, covering my head. I could feel myself leaking blood. My right pant leg was soaked. The pain was excruciating.

After what felt like minutes, but could only have been seconds, the British assassin stopped shooting. I waited, listening, heard nothing, and lifted my head. Casey Wu was gone.

"Damn, damn, damn," I cursed out loud. The pain in my leg was killing me. I hauled myself onto my feet, backed out of the room, pulled up my pant leg. The wound was tiny, through and through. It was bleeding, but not as much as I'd thought. *No big deal,* I thought, but I was wrong.

I went back into the locker room, then to the window and waved both arms, hoping the trigger-happy Brit would see me. I retrieved my Glock from the corner where it had landed and then limped back to the window and looked out. Nero had disappeared, no doubt going after Wu on his own. I'd lost her.

"Mrs. Hawke?" I shouted. "MaryAnne!"

"Here!" her muffled voice called from somewhere deep within the building.

"I'm coming!" I shouted, though I still had no idea where she was. I shouted again, "Where are you, MaryAnne?"

"Here... Please!" I now had the general direction and limped on, dripping blood.

Instead of going east along the staff hallway, I went the other way, between the kitchen and the lounge. I hadn't gone more than a dozen yards when I came to what I figured must once have been the kitchen pantry, a room maybe twenty feet by twenty. The pantry walls were covered with grime and graffiti. The floor was filthy and covered with the detritus of the past ten years: trash, beer cans, broken bottles, used condoms, needles, feces, and God only knew what else. It was dangerous just to be inside the room.

Off to the side of the pantry were three more doors.

"MaryAnne," I shouted. "Where are you?"

"In here!"

Her voice sounded out from behind the second door.

"Are you alone?"

"Yes, yes. She's gone. That woman has gone, Harry."

That woman, I thought. *What an odd choice of words.* "I'm coming in." And I did, my gun raised, but I holstered it when I saw her.

MaryAnne Hawke was in the center of a tiny walk-in closet, tied to a chair. She looked exhausted, miserable. Her face was white, her cheeks wet with tears. She looked up at me, her lower lip trembling. And then she burst out crying, tears streaming down her face as I untied her. Either she was genuinely happy to see me, or she was a complete sociopath. Something was telling me it was the latter.

"Thank you, thank you," she cried.

The nylon rope Wu had used to bind her wrists untangled easily, maybe too easily, and MaryAnne shook her hands as if to restore circulation.

"Did she hurt you?" I asked. "Are you okay?"

"Yes, I'm all right. She just tied me up, but I was scared. She said she'd kill me."

I nodded, watching her. She looked like a victim, and

she was acting like one, but I didn't trust her. I wasn't buying it.

"She won't," I assured her. "You were right when you said she was gone. My... colleague's in pursuit."

"Thank you again, Harry."

"There's no need to thank me," I replied, taking her hand. "Let's get out of here."

"You're bleeding," she said, but neither her voice nor her face showed any real concern. It was a statement, no more than that.

"It's just a scratch, don't worry about it."

She held my arm, steadying me, as we walked together through the trash to the lobby and then out into the sunshine.

I looked at my watch. It was almost ten o'clock; it felt later. I began to sweat in the heat of the sun. I hadn't showered in two days, nor had I changed my clothes: I was filthy...

"We need to get you to a hospital," MaryAnne said, holding my arm with both hands.

"Yeah, I know," I replied, and I reached into my pocket. *Shit.* "Do you have a phone?"

She shook her head. "It's at the trailer park."

"Of course, it is." I sighed, and then I swallowed. I was becoming dizzy. Whether it was the aftermath of the crap Nero had slipped into my drink the night before, or just the lack of sleep catching up with me, I had no idea. The injury to my leg wasn't helping either.

"We need to get to my car," I said, wincing.

"Okay. I'll help you. Where is it?"

"That way." I pointed.

As awkward as it felt, I had to put an arm around her

shoulder and she supported me as I half-hopped to my Maxima, fighting to stay upright.

I stripped off my holster and the vest, threw them onto the back seat, opened the driver's side door, and was about to get in when I felt her hand on my arm.

"You can't, Harry. You're in no condition."

I looked down at her. I was in no condition to argue either, so I nodded and pointed to the key still in the ignition. She nodded and helped me around to the passenger side. I opened the door and literally fell into the seat. For the second time that day, I had to let someone else drive. I managed to fasten the seat belt then laid back and stared out of the windshield.

"Do you know where to go?" I asked as she turned the key in the ignition.

"Vaguely," MaryAnne replied, her voice emotionless as she adjusted her seat and checked out the controls.

"Follow the road back to the gate, turn left, go about two miles, turn right onto the highway, then take the southbound ramp onto the Interstate and follow the signs." And then I closed my eyes.

Where the hell is Casey Wu? I wondered. *More to the point, where's Nero? What if...*

~

"Mr. Starke. Harry Starke," a faraway voice said, like a distant echo.

I ignored it.

"Mr. Starke!"

I woke up in a cold sweat. I was still in my car, in the passenger seat. The door was open and a police officer was standing over me, leaning into the car. I could hear the tick-tock of the Maxima's emergency lights, and the officer's crackling radio, and the sounds of cars speeding by outside.

"Are you all right, sir?"

"Yeah, yeah," I replied. I undid the seatbelt, leaned forward, and tried to get out of the car. I couldn't, so I just sat there, my feet outside the car on the asphalt.

The car was parked at the shoulder of I-75 mid-way between Bonny Oaks Drive and Shallowford Road, southbound into the city. A police cruiser was parked behind, its emergency lights flashing. A second cruiser was parked behind the first one.

I looked back and saw another officer questioning MaryAnne. She was standing beside the second cruiser. She was frowning, her arms folded.

"Sir, may I see your ID?"

"Sure," I said and raised my hands. "Back seat, inside jacket pocket. There's a weapon on the back seat and several more in the trunk."

The officer's eyes widened slightly, and he instinctively reached for his own gun.

"Just help yourself, officer," I said. "I'm so sleepy I can't see straight."

And he did.

The next ten minutes were spent trying to hold them off until the cavalry arrived, which it eventually did in the form of Kate Gazzara, an ambulance, another police cruiser, an FBI SUV, and an unmarked sedan driven by Agent Georgina Powell.

"Harry!" Kate called, as she ran toward me moments before the paramedics did.

"That'd be me, Sarge," I said, trying hard to smile. My

body was hurting all over, not to mention the damn bullet wound.

"Where the hell have you been? What the hell happened to you? You look like hell and you're bleeding like a pig."

"I'm fine, Kate, I swear," I said, glancing down at the blood beginning to pool around my right foot.

The paramedics picked me up and loaded me onto a gurney. As they wheeled me toward the ambulance, I saw MaryAnne Hawke climb into the black FBI SUV. Her husband leaned out, offering her a hand up, a fake smile plastered over his face...

30

I woke up that night in a hospital bed and wondered if it was the same hospital where they were treating Bob.

"He's asleep," Kate said from an armchair next to the bed, reading my mind.

"He's doing well, but they're keeping him through the weekend." She reached out and gently placed her hand on my arm. "I talked to him earlier. He's feeling much better now."

"I guess he's earned a couple of weeks of vacation. I need to get..." I tried to sit up. My leg was no longer hurting, but the rest of my body ached from the bruises and cuts. Even breathing was uncomfortable. I gave it up, lay back down, stared up at the ceiling, then turned my head and looked at Kate.

"Take it easy, Harry. You need to rest. You've had a rough couple of days."

You can say that again, I thought.

"How's MaryAnne?" I asked.

"She's holding up. Senator Hawke sends his eternal

gratitude. His words," she said, dryly, and smiled, but there was a touch of sadness to it. "I was so worried, Harry. I mean, I knew you'd do something stupid. You always do, but—"

"You didn't know just how stupid. Well, I like to think I'm full of surprises," I said, returning her smile. "C'mere."

She did, and we kissed. Her hair fell all over my face. It was wonderful. She smelled of flowers. And then she held me. That, too, was wonderful, except that it hurt like hell. I didn't complain.

"Can we go home?" I said.

"Depends on how you're feeling," she replied and kissed me again.

I put a hand on the back of her neck and held her close. "I'm feeling pretty good, right now."

"Oh, Lord. Okay, but at least let me lock the door," she said.

We did go home afterward, although I was still limping. The nurse said my wound was minor—yeah, for her— and that the bullet had missed the bone. It would be sore for a few days and I'd have to take antibiotics for a couple of weeks, but there was no permanent damage.

So Kate drove us home, and the first thing we did was take a long hot shower together. In moments like those, I always felt like I didn't need the damn job at all. And I didn't, at least not for the money. What kind of life was it anyway? A never-ending and ever-draining pursuit of scumbags.

Maybe I should settle down, have kids... Nah!

But that wasn't me, not then. The job... It wasn't exactly a calling, but it's what I did, what I do, and besides, Casey Wu was still out there; so was Nero, and the body count was rising. Booker and his driver brought the total to ten, and I still wasn't any closer to putting the people responsible behind bars.

"You're thinking about her, aren't you?" Kate said when we were drying off.

In any other context, between any other couple, those words would've preceded an argument. "You're not?" I said.

"MaryAnne's safe, Harry. The CPD will deal with Casey Wu and Nero. You can rest up."

"You know I can't." And I knew she knew. "Did you question her yet?"

"MaryAnne? About the kidnapping?" she asked.

"About the whole thing, Kate."

"You still think she's behind it?"

"I don't know. I'm not ruling it out, not until I know for sure. It's all just too... perfect," I said, not quite getting my feelings across. "Phony is maybe a better word."

I watched as she slipped one of my old T-shirts over her head. *Whew, how the hell did I get so lucky?*

"Perfect? Phony? She was almost killed."

"Was she? Or was it all part of her act?" I said, remembering how easy it had been to untie her.

"Have you ever considered that you might be overthinking it, Harry?"

I had. In fact, overthinking had always been part of the process. *Once you eliminate the impossible, what's possible*—and all that.

"If you think I'm overthinking it now, just wait until I tell you what I think about Senator Hawke's part in it."

She stared, but I only shrugged and went to the kitchen to pour myself some coffee, wondering. *What exactly do I think about Hawke, anyway?* The truth was, I didn't really know, not then, but I knew something wasn't right, that nothing, and I do mean nothing, was what it seemed to be.

Kate joined me in the kitchen. I poured coffee for her. She sat down on a barstool at the island.

"I'll need to talk to her, to Mrs. Hawke, in the morning. We can't let Casey Wu get away."

"Or Nero," Kate added, looking at me over the rim of her cup.

"Or Nero," I agreed, "but he's not our top priority."

"So you say, Harry, but I'm a cop; I've got a job to do."

"I know you do, but don't worry. If I'm right, it'll only make your job that much easier."

"What do you mean?" she asked.

"You'll see," I replied, unwilling to be drawn into yet another—*You can't do that, Harry*—conversation, both of us knowing full well I was going to do it anyway.

By noon we were both dressed and ready to leave. Me in dark blue pants, a freshly pressed white shirt, and my comfortable brown leather jacket Kate had thoughtfully retrieved from the back seat of my Maxima. It fit nicely over my shoulder holster and back-up M&P9; my car had been returned to me and was in my secure lot at the office, but the weapons had been seized.

Kate was wearing the same clothes she had on when she brought me home, a little crumpled, but she still looked fabulous in tight black jeans, a pale blue turtleneck, and a white leather shell jacket.

"Are you good to drive?" Kate asked as she drove me to my office.

"I'll manage," I said as we pulled in through the open gate. The street had been cleared of the wreckage of Booker's SUV, and only a slight discoloration of the office wall remained to remind us of what had happened less than thirty-six hours earlier.

"Good," Kate said. "We'll take your car."

We did, and she gave me the address of yet another safe house, one I knew well, where Agent Powell was keeping the Hawkes. Ten minutes later I parked the car in the multi-story lot next door to the Marriott Chattanooga Convention Center, beside an obviously FBI SUV.

"Not very subtle, right?" I said, patting the SUV on the hood.

Kate smiled but said nothing. She just led the way into the hotel. Once inside we took the elevator to the top floor and knocked on the door to the "safe house."

"What are you doing here, Mr. Starke?" SAIC Georgina Powell said when she opened the door and saw me.

Kate answered for me, "I invited him. We simply want to talk to Mrs. Hawke, to make sure that she's okay."

I thought for a minute she was going to refuse, but she didn't. Instead, she stepped to one side and let us in.

Far from the nasty trailer that Booker had set them up in, Powell had put the Hawkes in a luxury suite overlooking Lookout Mountain. It was a prime piece of Marriott real estate, much more fitting to the status of her charges.

Besides Powell, there were two more agents inside the room, both sitting within eyesight of the door. When I saw them, I had a sudden feeling of déjà vu and glanced back at the door, half-expecting it to burst open and for someone to start shooting. I was, of course, being stupid. Powell had chosen well. The suite was indeed safe.

"Are you all right, Harry?" Kate asked.

I nodded.

One of them patted us down; first Kate, then me. He stopped dead when he felt the weapon under my jacket. He grabbed the collar and pulled it aside, revealing the gun. Then he looked at Powell, his eyebrows raised. She nodded, and he stood back.

"Mr. Starke," Andrew Hawke said, rising to his feet from the couch where he'd been sitting with his wife. MaryAnne also stood.

He offered me his hand. I shook it. His grip was soft, like a dead octopus.

MaryAnne also offered me her hand, and I shook it. Her grip was strong and firm.

"MaryAnne," I said, "I'm glad to see you're holding up."

"All thanks to you," she replied. "And you look well-rested yourself. How's the leg?"

"Tis but a scratch," I said with a smile.

"To what do we owe the pleasure of your visit?" Hawke asked.

I opened my mouth to offer a lame excuse but thought better of it.

"I'd like... that is, we would like to talk to you both, if you don't mind."

They both hesitated. *Why?* I thought.

Hawke nodded and said, "Of course. Shall we sit?"

They both sat down again on the couch. I sat down opposite on a love seat; Kate sat next to me.

I decided to dive right in and said, "Mrs. Hawke, may we talk about yesterday?"

"Of course," she replied.

I turned to Powell. "Can we have a little privacy?"

The Agent jerked her head at the door, and her two agents left to stand outside and wait. Powell stayed with us, took a seat at the bar and listened. I turned back to MaryAnne.

"Why do you think Casey Wu decided to kidnap you, Mrs. Hawke?"

She looked at her husband, then at the two other women. We were all ears.

"She never said. Extortion, do you think?"

"Money?" I asked.

"Me," Senator Hawke replied. "She wanted me."

"Well, that's our theory," Powell said.

"Makes sense," I said. "She didn't harm you at all?"

MaryAnne shook her head.

"You don't find that suspicious?" I said, turning to Hawke.

"Mr. Starke?" Powell said.

"I don't under... stand," MaryAnne said, hesitantly. "What are you insinuating?"

"I'm simply trying to establish the facts."

There was a long pause, and then the Senator said, "I'll tell you what the facts are, Mr. Starke. Fact one: I don't like this line of questioning. MaryAnne was kidnapped by a killer for hire. I was the target. Fact two: you screwed up, and God knows how many people, including my best friend, are dead because of it. Fact three: you lost Casey Wu, who is probably going to attack us again. Fact four: I'm not sure your services will be needed any longer."

I held his gaze, trying to read the message in it. I knew for sure now that the Hawkes, both of them, were players in a game I wasn't qualified to play.

"I apologize," I said. "I've overstepped my boundaries, and I'm sorry that I've put you into this position. For what it's worth, I believe you should stay low for a while, definitely leave the state." I shrugged. "Just a thought."

Andrew Hawke frowned. "I don't think we will, Mr. Starke."

"No?" I feigned surprise.

"The Training Academy will reopen on Monday, and I plan to deliver another speech to the brave officers who protected us. What we can't afford to do is to hide. Isn't that so, MaryAnne?"

Hawke's wife nodded, narrowing her eyes at me.

I said, "That sounds very noble, Senator. I wish you the best of luck. I'll have Jacque send you an invoice for my time."

I put out my hand, and when neither of them shook it, I nodded and got up to leave. Both Kate and Powell stared at me in surprise, but I only shrugged.

At the door, Powell touched my elbow and said, "Don't leave town, Mr. Starke."

I grinned. "Wouldn't dream of it, Agent."

Kate took a minute to chat with Powell. I waited outside with the two agents, who largely ignored me. Kate joined me a moment later.

"What the hell were you thinking, Harry?" she asked as we took the elevator to the first floor. "I know you didn't just get yourself kicked off the case for laughs, so what's up?"

I told her my plan, and she listened, fascinated, but not happy.

"Oh shit!" She shook her head and rolled her eyes. "Another sting operation? Seriously?"

"Last one, I promise," I lied. "You have to admit, this one has only a small chance of going sideways."

I was confident it would work because this time I

knew all the players, their motivations, and how they operated. Sure, Wu and Nero were in the wind, but what else was new? Yes, it would be a little more difficult for me to get into the event now that I was technically "off the case," but I'd cross that bridge when I got to it.

"I suppose it could work," she said as we walked across the street to the parking garage. "I'll have to run it by Powell and the Chief, but either way, I can get you in. But Harry, surely MaryAnne wouldn't be crazy enough to try to kill her husband again?"

"Either she does, and we catch her, or she doesn't, and everyone will sleep in peace that night. Either way, we win, Kate."

We drove slowly out of the parking garage, still mulling it over. No sooner had we exited through the barrier than I saw something that made me hit the brake, and hard.

"Holy..." I was stunned.

We both stared ahead at the person blocking our exit from the parking garage.

"Oh, my God... really?" Kate muttered.

"He might as well be," I said.

Nero was standing on the sidewalk beside the exit onto Carter Street, his hands in his pockets like he was out for a stroll with not a care in the world. He was wearing blue jeans and a T-shirt, his face barely concealed by a pair of Ray-Ban Aviator sunglasses. He waved at us and walked over to my window. I shook my head, not believing what was happening. I rolled my eyes and then rolled the window down.

"Got room for one more?" Nero said.

I nodded, and he got in behind me.

Almost mindlessly, I turned right onto Carter Street toward the Highway 27 on-ramp.

I hadn't driven but fifty yards or so when he said, "Not a bad plan, guys. A tad, um, directionless, but we can work on that, tweak it a little."

The whole time, Kate was watching him, twisted in her seat. She said, "How did you find us?"

I answered for him. "He's got a tracker in my car."

I was watching him in the rear-view mirror.

He nodded, a devious smile on his lips.

"And you heard our conversation?" Kate said angrily.

"Yeah," I snapped. "How the hell—"

"I put a bug in your jacket, Harry."

"Of course, you did," I said, involuntarily glancing down at my traitorous jacket. "Where is it?"

"Inside pocket."

"Damn you, Nero," I said as I ran my fingers around inside the pocket. I found it, removed the tiny electronic device, and tossed it out the window.

"Hey," he said amiably. "There was no need for that. Those things are expensive. Now you owe me."

"Owe you, my ass," I said, now totally pissed off, but more than a little curious too.

"So what's wrong with my plan?" I asked. "How do you want to tweak it?"

"Well, riddle me this, guys. How do you plan to get Casey Wu to attend your little soiree?"

"I don't have to," I said. "MaryAnne Hawke will do that for me. She'll send her to kill hubby."

"Bloody hell! You think?" he asked derisively. "Wu's not a flippin' Muppet, Harry. She's ex-CIA. She won't risk it. Why would she?"

"Do you have a better idea?" I asked sarcastically.

Nero smirked. "Of course I do, don't I? I've got more than a better idea, actually. Hire me to work the event, and I guarantee you Casey will stick her neck out."

I looked at him in the rearview mirror, contemplating whether or not I should pull over and kick the nutjob out of the car.

Kate expressed my thoughts: "You're joking," she said, incredulous.

"Not at all," Nero said. "Casey doesn't give a shit about your senator or his wife, or their money. It's me she wants. I killed TSA, remember? She's mad as a dog, and we've got a chance to play her like a fiddle."

I drove on in silence. Nero said nothing more, giving us time to think about his proposition. The funny thing was, both Kate and I knew—at least I assumed she knew—he was right. Casey Wu was now a lone wolf with nothing left but to seek revenge. I'd seen her in action. She was good, she was committed, and she was deadly. But, knowing what I did of Nero, I knew he could handle her.

Holy cow, I thought. *I can't believe I'm saying this.*

"One condition."

"Yes?"

"You take Wu alive."

"At least until I can close the case and get her out of Chattanooga," Kate added. "Whatever you do after that is none of my business." She kicked back in the seat. "Lord, I can't believe I'm even considering it. I have a lot to think about..."

"Where to, Albert?" I said.

31

We spent the next three days in preparation. As before, we had two schemes going at the same time.

The first one, on the surface, was the tougher of the two.

How the hell she'd managed it, I still don't know, but Kate had managed to convince Powell and the powers that be to give Albert Westwood immunity and employ him as a security consultant for Andrew Hawke's speech at the Academy—on the promise that he would testify against Casey Wu. My thought was that either Powell was nuts or she would do just about anything to bring Wu in, dead or alive.

The Hawkes? That was another surprise. Instead of arguing about it, they welcomed his presence. They even thanked him for what he did at the trailer park and at the drive-in. I believe the tag MaryAnne used was, "our personal guardian angel."

It was a go, but it wasn't all honey. Powell interviewed Nero extensively, but finally agreed to let him attend the event, but here's the kicker: he was to go unarmed and would be accompanied at all times by three FBI agents.

"Piece of cake," he told us later.

The story was strategically leaked to the press, who did the rest for us. The news spread like wildfire: Ex-British Special Forces Assassin to Protect Senator Hawke. Okay, it was a bit over-the-top, but it wasn't completely bogus.

We agreed that Nero's primary objective would be to flush out Wu, no more than that. Hah, but I knew different.

It sounded simple enough, but I had to wonder if Senor Murphy and his law would rear his ugly head one last time.

While Nero was concentrating his efforts on Wu, I would be running my own sting operation. My goal was to catch MaryAnne Hawke in the act, but of what exactly? As the Assistant District Attorney, Larry Spruce, informed me, direct contact between MaryAnne and Casey Wu would, by itself, be only circumstantial evidence. They could be meeting about anything. A lot would depend upon the nature of that contact. There had to be no question as to the intent. A direct order to kill Andrew Hawke, for instance, would be a slam dunk. And getting that would depend on a lot of things, none of them pleasant for Hawke himself, and certainly not good for his run for office.

And if we did manage to catch Wu, that in itself would be a win.

On the Monday that the event was to take place, Agent Powell, along with three black, unmarked SUVs, and Sergeant Kate Gazzara with two blue and white cruisers, arrived at The Marriot Chattanooga Convention

Center and blocked off the entrance to the hotel and the parking garage, posting guards every fifty feet around the complex. Nobody could get in or out. The media would call it an example of the incredible cooperation between the FBI and the CPD.

Agent Powell and Detective Gazzara met the Hawkes in their top-floor suite. The blinds were shut tight and agents were posted at the elevator doors, in the hallway, and outside the Hawkes' room.

"All set, Senator?" Powell asked.

"I believe so, Agent," he replied and gave Kate a confident nod.

The Senator wore a navy suit with no tie, while Mary-Anne wore a black dress cut just above the knee, with red shoes and a clutch purse to match.

The four of them took the elevator to the first floor and boarded the largest of the three SUVs, and the procession rolled out onto Carter Street, a CPD cruiser leading the way, and another bringing up the rear.

~

Albert Westwood had arrived at the new Police Academy an hour earlier and had checked in at the reception desk in Building A, where he received a visitor's pass, which made him smile: no running around in the forest this time. He wasn't alone, either: he was escorted, per the agreement, by the three FBI agents whose job it was to watch his every move. They were authorized to use brute force, even lethal force to restrain him, if it proved necessary, courtesy of SAIC Georgina Powell.

Westwood was not at all bothered by his escort. He'd

dealt with greater odds many times over the years. But he smiled politely and kept his hands where they could see them.

"No monkey business, lads," he said with a grin.

The men didn't reply. They led him to Building B, and they took the elevator to the top floor—where we'd decided to keep him—to a room overlooking the stadium, just down the hall from the one where Simon Wilder had been killed.

Westwood stepped over to the window, looked out, and smiled when he saw the devastation he'd caused: the charred remains of the sheds he'd blown up as part of his diversion. Most of it had been cleaned up, of course, but enough still remained to bring a smile to his lips.

As to the stadium itself, the stage was set much as it had been a week earlier. Three hundred folding chairs in three blocks of one hundred had been set up in front of it, also much as before, and they were already filled to capacity.

Because of the attempt on the Senator's life, the inaugural class at the Academy had been delayed by a week. That he'd returned to try again was no surprise to anyone, not even the media. After all, it's what we do, right? Bounce back in the face of adversity, especially when you're running for office... Not. But Hawke was a politician, so it was exactly what he would do.

The Hawkes arrived shortly before noon to be greeted by an excited, cheering crowd. The VIP group was escorted to the stage surrounded by a ring of FBI agents. Senator Hawke and MaryAnne waved and smiled all the way to the stage where they were greeted by the head of the Academy, while the host—a young female recruit in police uniform—introduced the guests to raucous applause.

Westwood shook his head and smiled. It was, he thought, as if they were welcoming a hero home from the war. And, in a way, I guess they were; many of the people in the audience that day had also been there the previous week, when the Senator almost lost his life.

Albert Westwood continued to watch the event unfold from his vantage point on the top floor of Building B, but he had little interest in the proceedings on stage; he had more important things to think about.

He turned around, his back to the window, hands in his pants pockets, observing his escorts. Two of the agents were seated by the door, the other was lounging comfortably in an armchair, his fingers steepled together, watching him, smiling at him; there was nothing friendly about the smile. It was one of those "gotcha" kind of looks. Westwood grinned. All three continued to watch him, silently. There were also two more agents stationed outside the door, but Westwood didn't know that.

"Enjoying your assignment, lads?" he asked, but no one replied.

"Didn't think so. Babysitting? Ugh." He grinned. "Better stay alert, though. Wu's coming for you."

Outside, Senator Hawke began his speech, thanking everyone for their service, congratulating the officers of the police department on how well they'd dealt with the threat of the previous week, blah, blah, blah. He talked about how much Chattanooga and the state of Tennessee meant to him and how much he intended to do for its people, should he be elected governor. Westwood yawned.

Suddenly, Agent Armchair's hand shot to his ear.

"Roger that," he said and rose to his feet.

"Stay put, sir," he ordered Westwood, sternly.

Westwood shrugged but did as he was told.

Agent Armchair stepped over to his colleagues and they spoke together, their voices low.

"She's here, isn't she?" Westwood said. "Told ya." The agents glanced at him, and he mouthed, "Ooohh!"

"Sir, don't move," one of the agents said, as Agent Armchair put a hand on his gun.

Westwood didn't flinch. Holding his hands up shoulder high, he took a tentative step toward the agents. They tensed. All three of them had their hands on their weapons.

He took another step.

"Mr. Westwood, this is your last warning."

"It is?" Westwood smirked.

The guns were out—three Sig Sauer P226s, all pointed at his chest. He took another step.

"Let me spell it out for you, boys," he said, his hands still up. "Casey Wu is not here to kill the Senator. She's here to kill *me*. To get to me, she has to get past you guys. To do that, she has to kill you, and she won't think twice about doing so. So, why don't you just let me go, and I'll make sure that doesn't happen."

"Can't do that," Armchair said.

Westwood sighed, shook his head, looked down at Armchair's feet, and said, "Fair enough."

Then, Westwood took a quick step forward, his left hand shot out, grabbed Armchair's wrist, pulling him toward him, while his right hand snatched the Sig and pointed it at the agent's face, the muzzle only inches from his nose. All three men were taken totally by surprise.

"Steady on now, gents," Westwood said amiably,

using Armchair as a shield from the other two. "Let's try this again."

The two agents looked at him. He could see the indecision in their eyes.

"C'mon, fellas," he said, "it's not too late. Just move away from the door, okay?"

But when they didn't move, he said, "You had your chance. Drop your weapons or I'll put this lovely man on sticks for the rest of his days."

He took a half-step back and pointed the Sig at the agent's right knee. They hesitated.

"On three, then," he said, quietly and began to count: "one..."

They dropped their guns.

"Kick 'em over here and step back." They did.

"Turn around. Stand over there, face against the wall." They did as he said.

"You," he said to Armchair. "Tie them up. Move slowly."

"With what?"

"The zip ties you brought for me, ducky," he said sarcastically.

Armchair stared at him, then carefully stepped sideways, picked up his briefcase from beside his chair, opened it, took out the ties, and stepped over to his colleagues.

"Careful, now. No sudden moves if you want to be able to continue walking. That's it," he said as he watched the zip pulled tight around the second agent's wrists.

"Good! Now tie them together... Come on, mate, quickly. We don't have much time."

When Armchair was finished, the two agents were standing back-to-back, joined together at the wrists.

"Now, turn around and face the wall," he told Armchair.

Without looking away from the man, Westwood stepped close to him and said, "So sorry," and then hit Armchair on the back of the head with the flat of the barrel. The man collapsed at his feet.

"You two," Westwood said as he twitched his head, covering them with the gun, "over there and sit down."

They shuffled sideways over to the couch and sat down.

"Stay put, lads, and all will be well," Westwood said, then turned and walked out of the room, straight into the arms of the other two guards.

"Freeze!" they shouted.

And he did, raising his hands above his head, the Sig still in his right hand.

There was a ding at the end of the hallway and the elevator doors opened. Casey Wu strode out, an M4 assault rifle in her hands. Without a word of warning, she opened fire, hitting one of the agents and splintering the doorframe.

Westwood took a step back into the room, bullets from the M4 shredding the door frame. He listened, waiting for her to run out of ammo. It was, of course, impossible to count the shots, but then all went quiet. He heard a click and stepped out into the corridor just as her magazine hit the floor.

"Too bad, Casey," he shouted. "You lose."

He fired once, hitting her in the right shoulder, sending her spinning backward, the M4 flying out of her hands. She collapsed to her knees, her arms hanging loosely at her sides.

He began to walk toward her. She stared at him, her eyes filled with hate, and with her left hand she—

"Damn it, Casey," Westwood snarled.

He shot her again, in the left shoulder. Her gun, a vintage Beretta M-71 .22 semi-automatic pistol dropped from her fingers, and she fell over sideways.

He stood over her as she lay half on her back on the floor, bleeding profusely. He pointed the Sig at her face, his finger on the trigger.

"I should kill you, Casey," he said in a low voice, his face pale. "After all you've done... D'you think for a minute that I forgot about Bucharest?"

His finger tightened on the trigger. Casey stared up at him, unafraid.

For a long moment he stood there, the gun steady in his hand, then he said, "You can thank Harry Starke for your life." And he tossed the weapon, stepped around her, and walked away.

Minutes later, Building B was swarming with cops, drawn by the sound of the shooting on the top floor, but by then Albert Westwood, also known as Nero, had disappeared.

32

When the agents on the ground, in the stadium, and on the stage with the Senator and his wife, heard the gunfire, they hustled the Hawkes off the stage and into an SUV parked just to the rear. With tires screeching and its engine roaring, the big car left the stadium and the complex in a cloud of dust. Forty-five minutes later, the Hawkes were back in their room at the Marriott Convention Center.

Agent Powell had feared that Wu might not be working alone, that there might be a second shooter lurking somewhere in the Academy complex. But, as I would learn later, Wu was indeed acting alone that day, and it was Nero she was after, not Andrew Hawke.

It was over. Casey Wu was badly injured, but she would live. She was in the ICU at Erlanger under twenty-four-hour watch. Albert Westwood was long gone, as I expected him to be.

Senator Hawke seemed unaffected by his second close call and relieved to learn the nightmare was finally over. But, as they rode the elevator to the top floor of the luxury hotel, MaryAnne Hawke did not look quite so pleased. The agents escorting them who noted the look on her face, didn't pay it much attention. Emotional support for the Hawkes wasn't part of their job description. Even Agent Powell respectfully looked away, trying to afford the couple at least the illusion of privacy.

The elevator dinged, and they stepped out into the hallway and made their way to their room. Once they were safely inside, Agent Powell asked if they needed anything before she left them alone.

"Just some rest, and a drink, I think, Agent," Hawke said. "Thank you for everything. I'm extremely grateful for all you've done."

"Very well, Senator," she said. "I'll leave you, then. My people will be posted outside all night, so you can rest easy. I'm told Agent Wu was taken to the hospital, but she is alive and responsive. We'll be talking to her shortly."

"Thank you again, Agent Powell," Hawke said, and he shook her hand.

MaryAnne ignored them both and went to the bathroom.

Andrew Hawke took four miniatures—one vodka and three scotch—from the mini-bar, poured all three scotches into a tumbler, downed half of it, and then poured the vodka into a separate glass.

MaryAnne stepped out of the bathroom, and he handed her the vodka. Together they shared a half-hearted toast.

"To us, Annie," Hawke said. "It's over."

"Almost," she said.

"What do you mean?"

She didn't reply. Instead, she walked to the bed where her red clutch lay, where she'd tossed it when she entered the suite. She set the vodka glass on the nightstand, picked up the clutch, and began to rummage through it.

"Looking for this?" Hawke asked, holding up a Ruger LCR 38 Special, a small five-shot revolver, light and compact, the perfect size for a woman's bag.

MaryAnne froze. "What are you doing, Andrew?" she asked, the color drained from her face.

"I know what you did, MaryAnne," he said easily, the revolver hanging by the trigger guard from the index finger of his right hand. "I know you hired those killers."

"That's absurd!" she snapped. "Who gave you that idea? That damned detective, Starke? Whoever it was, they're lying to you. Andy, I love you. You know that."

Hawke chuckled. "Now that I don't believe. The thing is, though, I do love you, which is why this is going to be difficult for me." He flipped the gun around on his finger, the grip landing firmly in the palm of his hand, his finger now on the trigger.

Her expression hardened: her eyes narrowed to mere slits. "You... you fricking asshole. You absolute power-hungry... monster! You think you can kill me and get away with it?"

"Yes, actually, I do. But, power-hungry? A monster? Isn't that quite rich, MaryAnne, especially coming from a politician's wife who ordered a hit on him?"

"Is that all I am to you, Andrew? A politician's wife? Oh, don't bother to answer. I already know what you think."

She stepped closer to him, forcing him to raise the gun slightly. She ignored it.

"I've spent thirty years in your shadow, Andy. You're such a self-centered, arrogant piece of shit. I should've hired someone to kill you much sooner."

Hawke raised the pistol, pointed it at her face, and said, "Me too, darling. Me too."

∽

By now you must be wondering, *Harry, you weren't there, so how do you know all this?* Well... let me walk you through it.

Three minutes after the Hawkes had left the Marriott on their way to the Academy, I went down the hallway to the suite next door to the Hawkes. Naturally, I was stopped along the way by an FBI agent whose job it was to guard the hallway.

I gave him a number to call, and soon after, Kate Gazzara informed him that Harry Starke was a consultant for the CPD, as was IT expert, Tim Clarke. Tim had been released from the hospital the day prior.

Five minutes after I entered the room, Tim joined me, grinning like a fool and trailing a rollaboard suitcase. While I watched, he spent the next thirty minutes setting up his equipment, and then we sat back, relaxed, and waited.

∽

"Goodbye, MaryAnne," Hawke said, his finger tightening on the trigger.

And that's when I burst in through the adjoining door that separated the two suites, my Smith and Wesson trained on the Senator.

"Drop the gun, Senator," I ordered.

Hawke, momentarily taken aback, turned, then saw me and smiled. "Well, well. Mr. Starke. What a surprise. I must admit. Well played, Harry, but it's too late, I'm afraid."

"It's not, Senator. Drop the gun, and we'll talk."

"No need, Harry. People will be talking about it soon enough, on the evening news. They'll talk about MaryAnne Hawke's attempt to poison her husband, and how he had to protect himself."

"What are you talking about?" I asked, and I could see by her expression that MaryAnne was wondering the same thing.

Andrew Hawke staggered slightly, the gun waving a little. Then he seemed to gather himself, brought the gun to bear again on his wife.

"You lost, Starke," he whispered.

"Do something!" MaryAnne screamed.

And I did. From six feet, it was an easy shot. I hit Hawke in the upper right arm. He spun. The gun flew out of his fingers and landed on the bed. He slammed into the mini-bar, and then fell to the floor, unconscious.

MaryAnne jumped backward several feet, her hands to her mouth, and then she shouted, "Did you see what he tried to do? He was going to kill me. Oh, my God."

I didn't reply. By then both Agent Powell and Kate Gazzara and their agents and officers had flooded the room. The Senator, still unconscious, and MaryAnne were handcuffed, and she was led away, protesting noisily. Paramedics were called while Powell yelled for people to clear the room.

Me? I ignored the commotion and stepped back through the adjoining door into the next-door suite where Tim was rolling back the video footage he'd captured of the Hawkes' argument.

"Good job, kid," I said, patting him on the back.

"Ouch!"

"Sorry." I smiled. "I'll leave you to it."

~

"So, it turned out they were both psychos, huh?" Bob asked, several days later. He was in a wheelchair, in my office. He looked much better than he had when he was released from the hospital the previous Monday morning, the same day the Hawkes were arrested. He was still a little pale, and he didn't make too much of a scene when the nurse that accompanied him insisted he remain in the wheelchair for the duration of his visit.

"I wouldn't call them psychos," I said. "Just... politicians."

"Well, I'm glad you were able to take care of them without me, Harry."

"Yeah, someone has to do the work while you're on vacation! But how's your chest feeling?"

"Like it's been stabbed with a knife, dumbass."

We both chuckled, and then I wheeled him out of my office and down the hall to the conference room, where Kate along with the rest of my team—Ronnie, Jacque, and Tim, and even Heather Stillwell—were gathered around the table for a small, but happy celebration. The girls kissed Bob on the cheeks; the guys shook his hand.

"Looking good, man," Ronnie said.

I tapped Kate on the shoulder and nodded for her to follow me to my office.

"So," I said, "have you spoken to the Chief yet? How about Agent Powell? How's she taking it? More to the point, what are they going to do about me?"

"Oh, Harry, you're Teflon. Without you... wow," and she began to list all of the things that might have been.

I grabbed her, planted my lips on hers, stopping her in full flow. She resisted, but only for a minute, then she threw her arms around my neck and...

"The whole thing's an incredible mess," she said, breathlessly, as we untangled ourselves. "They've been grilling Wu constantly ever since she was taken into custody, but she's not talking. They say they're going to transfer her to Nashville. Out of sight, out of mind, I guess."

I kissed her again, and we held each other for a long moment, then we rejoined the others in the conference room. Kate bent down and hugged Bob, whispered goodbye in his ear, then turned to me and said, "I should go. Police business."

"I bet. My place tonight?" I asked.

"If you promise to make it worth my time," she said and winked.

I winked back at her and nodded.

She said the rest of her goodbyes and left.

I accompanied Bob and his nurse outside to the parking lot, where his wheelchair-accessible van was waiting.

It was then I noticed a small envelope tucked under the windshield wiper on the driver's side of my Maxima. Curious, I grabbed it and then went to the van to say goodbye to Bob.

"What's that?" he asked.

"Let's find out."

The envelope was plain, about the size of a small greeting card, the kind you'll find attached to a bouquet of flowers. It wasn't sealed, so I opened it and extracted a small handwritten note.

It read: *I'll say hi to Casey for you. Cheers, mate.*

I laughed out loud. Bob stared at me, confused. I handed the note to him.

He read it, looked up at me, and said, "Son of a bitch. What the hell does it mean, exactly?"

"Only time will tell," I replied, shaking my head.

And time did tell, but that's another story.

FREE BOOK

"Genesis, a sure to be bestseller and 5-star action mystery-thriller and find out for yourself - what are you waiting for?" *Rosemary- Amazon Reviewer*

Would you like a free copy of the first book in my new best-selling Harry Starke series, Genesis? Just sign up for my newsletter and I'll send you a copy. Click Here to join.

ACKNOWLEDGMENTS

Many people have helped with the writing of this book, and I thank them all, especially my editor Diane Shirke. Great job Diane.

My thanks go also to my friends still in law enforcement and retired, for their help in the past and the present... and for the help I know you'll provide in the future, especially you Ron, Gene, David and Richard.

Thanks also to my Beta readers who managed to find most of those annoying little typos.

Finally, thanks to my ever-patient wife, Jo... and of course to my constant companion, even if she does eat everything that's not tied down, Sally, my Jack Russell Terrier.

ONE MORE THING

Thank you:

I hope you enjoyed reading this story as much as I enjoyed writing it. If you did, I really would appreciate it if you would take just a minute to write a brief review on Amazon (just a sentence will do).

Here's the link. It will take you to the Amazon page and then you just scroll down and you'll find the place to post. So, to post a review Click Here. It will work wherever in the world you might be. And thank you:

Reviews are so very important. I don't have the backing of a major New York publisher. I can't take out ads in newspapers or on TV, but you can help get the word out. I would be very grateful if you would spend just a couple of minutes and post a review.

If you have comments or questions, you can contact me by e-mail at blair@blairhoward.com, and you can visit my website http://www.blairhoward.com.

Finally, I'd like to invite you to sign up for my newsletter. I send out just a couple of short reads a month – eh, maybe a couple more when I'm releasing a new novel -

along with offers of free books from me and fellow authors, news about what I'm doing, and my new releases. NO SPAM EVER. I promise. Please Click Here to get my newsletter, and thank you so much.

Blair Howard, November 2019

Made in the USA
Middletown, DE
07 May 2020